ALSO BY JUDITH BLEVINS

Double Jeopardy
Swan Song
The Legacy
Karma

ALSO BY CARROLL MULTZ

Justice Denied
Deadly Deception
License to Convict
The Devil's Scribe
The Chameleon
Shades of Innocence

ALSO BY JUDITH BLEVINS
& CARROLL MULTZ

Rogue Justice

So throw off the bowlines.
Sail away from the safe harbor.
Catch the trade winds in your sails.
Explore. Dream. Discover.

~ MARK TWAIN ~

THE
PLAGIARIST
a novel of suspense

JUDITH BLEVINS &
CARROLL MULTZ

OPEN WINDOW
Livonia, Michigan

Cover design, interior book design, and eBook design
by Blue Harvest Creative
www.blueharvestcreative.com

Published by Open Window
an imprint of BHC Press

Library of Congress Control Number:
2016959280

ISBN-13: 978-1-946006-24-0
ISBN-10: 1-946006-24-6

Visit the authors at:
www.bhcpress.com

TABLE OF CONTENTS

A NOTE FROM THE AUTHORS

Our second adult novel as co-authors is truly a collaborative effort as was the first. Unsure we could duplicate the feat, we did so with relative ease. After our seven young adult novels, collaboration has become the rule rather than the exception. And, the adage that two heads are better than one, has proven to be true once again.

As with all our novels, *The Plagiarist* is designed to inspire, inform and entertain in that order. The theme of our new novel is that to take ideas, writings, etc. from another and pass them off as one's own is never acceptable and comes with a price. *Once burned— twice learned!*

We wish to express our appreciation to Gary and Shirley Carr, Margie Vollmer Rabdau and our publisher, BHC Press, for their editing skills and technical assistance.

Dedicated to the incorruptible.

PROLOGUE

B
ut, I am telling you the truth..." I stammer.

"Sure, sure. That's what they all say," Detective Blake Corrigan responds.

I detect skepticism in his voice. *He doesn't believe me!* I drop my head into my hands, covering my face. I'm barely able to grasp what's happening. *How did I come to this...this...this nightmare?*

I'm cuffed to a metal ring embedded in the steel table in a dank, smelly interrogation room at the Coral Cove police station. Corrigan, my interrogator, looks up at the officer who is standing beside me, "Book him, Jackson, murder one." Corrigan then roughly slams closed the three ring binder that has been lying on the table between us; it was opened to a picture of the victim laying in a pool of blood. The binder is labeled LISETTE KINGSTON MURDER INVESTIGATION.

Corrigan tucks the binder under his arm as he noisily scoots his chair back and stands. Turning, he lifts his windbreaker from the back of the chair with his forefinger and causally tosses it over his shoulder. "I'm going home," he announces and starts for the door.

The finality of that statement unnerves me. "WAIT!" I shout. "You don't understand..."

"Tell it to the judge, Donovan, maybe he'll be more understanding." Corrigan is at the door in two strides, but before he exits, he turns and says, "I gave you a chance to come clean, now I'm done with you."

As the door slams shut behind him, so does any hope I have of ever convincing anyone of what really happened. If I hadn't lived it, I wouldn't believe it either.

1

CAST OFF

Reclining in one of the lounge chairs, I bask in the cool, crisp January morning. The panoramic view of the Atlantic is spectacular from the redwood deck of my parents' Key West oceanfront home. Dad and I plan to dive this morning, and as I wait for him, I reflect on how lucky I am to be alive at this time and in this place. This is the last week of winter break and when I return to school, I'll be starting my final semester as a graduate student at Wellington York University.

I'm known as "Cam" to those near and dear to me. However, my given name is Cameron Louis Donovan. My parents, Wayne and Michelle Donovan, are native Floridians and have lived in the Keys all of their lives. Dad is a successful real estate broker and because keeping erratic business hours comes with the turf, he is gone much of the time. Mom, in order to combat the boredom of being alone so often, purchased a quaint little curio shop which she renamed *Shelly's Sea Shells*.

Dad comes from a long line of mariners. However, fishing is not his sport. He prefers recreational diving and not one to let an

13

opportunity slip past, he used Mom's shop as an excuse to purchase a yacht which he christened *Pizzazz*. The family joke is that the purchase was "to keep Michelle supplied with exotic shells."

I virtually grew up on *Pizzazz* as Dad started taking me to sea as soon as I was out of diapers—that was some twenty-two years ago. He educated me on ships from stem to stern and taught me how to swim, dive, navigate and of course, how to find and harvest the best shells.

I LOOK UP as Dad approaches. His diving gear is slung over one shoulder and as he adjusts the weight of the oxygen tank, asks, "Ready, Son?"

"You bet!" I answer. Standing, I gather my equipment from the picnic table and fall in alongside Dad. We descend the redwood steps and shuffle through the sand the short distance to the pier where Dad keeps *Pizzazz* moored.

Nearing the jetty, I detect soft splashing sounds as the craft gently rocks against the string of old tires that line the dock. I shield my eyes with my hand and look up as a flock of squawking seagulls soar overhead.

"DAMN VULTURES!" Dad shouts and whips his Miami Marlins baseball cap from his head and swings it wildly at the birds. "We'll most likely be cursed with their company the rest of the day."

"Little beggars, probably just looking for a handout," I jab, knowing how much Dad dislikes the gulls.

"HUMPH!" Dad snarls and puts his cap back on. Still scouring the sky, he says, "Weather looks good and after the recent storms, if we hit it just right, we can count on a pretty good harvest today."

When we reach the vessel's moor at the end of the pier, Dad leans down and pulls the tethering rope tight snuggling *Pizzazz* against the protective line of tires. He braces one foot against her hull, steadying the craft long enough for me to heave our diving gear aboard.

Dad then unties the tether and still holding the length of rope in one hand, he hands me the keys with the other. He then jerks his head toward the bridge, "Go ahead and start 'er up, Cam."

"Aye, aye, Sir!" I respond and gingerly vault over the port railing and head for the bridge. Slipping onto the captain's chair, I insert the key into the ignition and feel the vibration of the powerful Evinrude as it roars to life. I expect no less; Dad takes better care of *Pizzazz* than most men do their wives.

HOWEVER, NOT ALL of my lessons came easily. At the tender age of ten, not unlike most kids, I thought I knew everything—that is up until the day I almost drowned. Dad and I were diving a few miles off the southern tip of Key West. Enchanted by the coral reefs and colorful tropical fish indigenous to the area, I was preoccupied by my surroundings and not paying much attention to what I was doing. As I swam along a few feet above the ocean floor, I suddenly realized that my right flipper had become entangled in the net we were using to collect our harvest.

Try as I may, I couldn't free my foot. I began to thrash about stirring up a cloud of sand, impairing my vision. Not being able to see clearly, I blundered into a nearby coral reef scraping my legs on the sharp spiny outgrowths. As blood seeped from the wounds, I panicked at the thought that sharks could be roaming nearby and I become even more violent in my endeavors to free my foot. I twisted and turned jerking my body this way and that way, depleting my oxygen supply in the process. In my anxiety, I did all the wrong things.

Although it seemed to me like an eternity, Dad was almost instantly at my side. He took my face in both of his hands forcing me to look at him and shook his head indicating for me to calm down. Dad's presence reassured me and once I was under control, Dad pulled the knife from his diving belt and made several swift slices through the net thus releasing my foot. Even as traumatized as I was, I knew better than to ascend too quickly so once free, I slowly floated upward. When we were both safely aboard *Pizzazz,* Dad seized the opportunity to lecture me on the necessity of remaining calm, especially underwater, and especially in time of peril.

Embarrassed, I replied, "I know that, Dad, but, but...my only thought was that I was going to die."

"And Cam, you probably would have because you panicked." Dad heaved a sigh and pushing his wet hair back from his forehead, he said, "In a way I'm glad that your first real crisis happened on my watch. At least *this* time, I was there to help you."

I felt myself blush, embarrassed by my *faux pas.* "Thanks, Dad," I said and slumped onto the deck. I didn't want to think of the alternative.

Dad smiled and reached over and tousled my hair. "Next time and, mark my words, Cam, there will be a next time, you'll be better prepared for the emergency."

I nodded, but, still unnerved from my brush with death, I silently vowed there wouldn't be a next time, not if I could help it. And, if there was, I'd be prepared.

Once we recovered from the scare, we hauled the now almost empty net aboard. Most of the shells had escaped through the cut portion on the way to the surface. When we had the net secured, we spread it out on the deck in order to assess the damage.

Looking it over, Dad said, "Well, Son, it's not too bad." Then, pointing to the cut portion, he said, "To make sure you remember this day, you get to mend the net."

I groaned. Mending net was my least favorite shipboard duty. However, relieved to still be alive, I gratefully accepted my punishment as consequences of my own actions. I stood and with a stiff salute, replied, "Aye, aye, Captain Sir!" Dad laughed and returned my salute.

TODAY, I STAND on the bridge alongside Dad as he navigates *Pizzazz* through familiar channels. I watch the shoreline fade into the distance and when we're far enough out, I retreat to the stern, slip into my wetsuit and check my gear preparing for the dive.

As soon as I'm set, I approach the bridge. "I'm good to go," I say to Dad.

Dad looks up and gestures for me to take the controls. "You drive 'er, Son, while I change."

I take the helm and as we plow through the sea, we're baptized with an occasional spray of salt water. I look back and, as I watch Dad struggle into his wet suit, my heart overflows with love for that man. Reflecting back over my childhood, I realize I will always and forever cherish the times we spent together on *Pizzazz* but following in Dad's footsteps is not my heart's desire.

MY PASSION IS to become a writer and I have designed my education around achieving that goal with a dual major in Journalism and English. Wellington York offers graduate journalism majors the rare opportunity to mentor with a published author during the student's last semester. Each year, at the end of the fall term, a list is posted with the names of private-sector volunteers who are willing to shepherd a student apprentice. The student will be under the tutelage of his or her mentor the final semester in lieu of attending classes.

It's December and the fall semester is almost complete when the list is posted. I immediately zero in on a local author, Ashland Prescott. Prescott's four mystery novels have been on the New York Times Bestseller list. I have read all of them and they are among my favorites. I can't believe my luck and needless to say, I instantly apply for the internship. I soon receive a reply to my letter and to my delight, Mr. Prescott accepts my application. The return letter I receive reads:

Ashland Prescott
P.O. Box 1936
Coral Cove, FL 33002

Mr. Cameron Donovan
c/o Wellington York University
Drawer 2895
Fort Lauderdale, FL 33120

Dear Mr. Donovan:

Dean Wesley Attenborough forwarded me the application you submitted requesting admittance to the writer's internship program. Dr. Attenborough expressed that, in his opinion, you would be an excellent candidate for an internship.

Upon reviewing your credentials, I echo Dr. Attenborough's opinion. I would be pleased to be your mentor during the upcoming spring semester.

This internship comes at a fortunate time in both of our lives as I'm just beginning a new novel and, as an intern, you would be involved in the writing from beginning to end. That, in and of itself, is a rare opportunity as usually my novels are well underway before the internship program commences.

In accordance with Wellington York's policy, interns are expected to live in close proximity to their mentor. My oceanfront home is spacious and therefore, I have adequate room to accommodate you if you wish to live here during your last semester. The tradeoff is I'm in need of a typist; my current typist informed me she is working on a thesis and needs to devote her time to its completion before the end of the spring term. Sadly enough, I must admit that my computer skills are virtually nonexistent. My offer to you is that you type my manuscript in exchange for room and board.

Please let me know as soon as possible if this arrangement is agreeable to you.

Regards,
Ashland Prescott
np

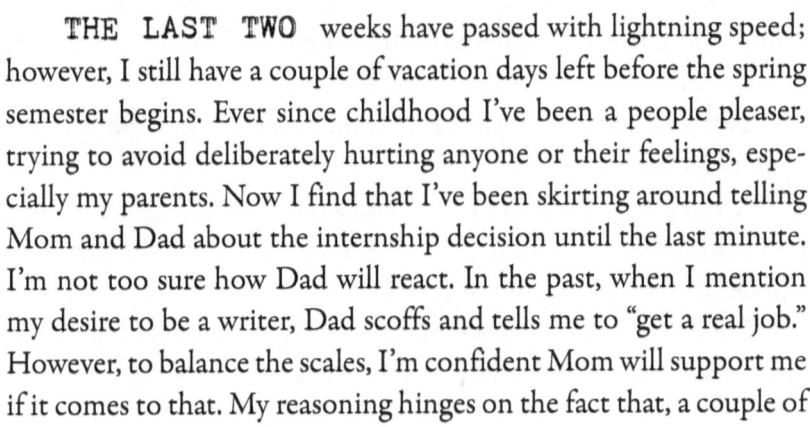

THE LAST TWO weeks have passed with lightning speed; however, I still have a couple of vacation days left before the spring semester begins. Ever since childhood I've been a people pleaser, trying to avoid deliberately hurting anyone or their feelings, especially my parents. Now I find that I've been skirting around telling Mom and Dad about the internship decision until the last minute. I'm not too sure how Dad will react. In the past, when I mention my desire to be a writer, Dad scoffs and tells me to "get a real job." However, to balance the scales, I'm confident Mom will support me if it comes to that. My reasoning hinges on the fact that, a couple of years ago when I mentioned to Mom why my majors were in Journalism and English, she confided in me that she had always had a desire to write. This revelation surprised me since it had never been mentioned and I had no idea. *Guess writing is in the blood!*

This afternoon Mom and I are alone on the deck sorting shells when I broach the subject of my internship. Mom stops her sorting and looks out over the ocean. I follow her gaze. We watch the setting sun paint the underbelly of the clouds various shades of pink as it bids the eastern half of the U.S. goodnight.

Mom sits toying with a small gold cross, a permanent fixture fastened around her neck on a delicate gold chain. I recognize that this gesture is something she does when she's conflicted. Finally, she says, "It must be in your genes," and her smile encourages me to continue.

"Must be...but...but, Dad has his heart set on my partnering with him after I graduate." Then after a pause, I ask, "How do you think *he'll* react?"

Mom covers my hand with hers, "Not well I suspect, but he'll get over it. I'm sure he realizes you don't want to waste your education chasing the real estate circus." She gently squeezes my hand and adds, "You follow *your* heart, Cam, not your Dad's or mine."

I nod. We sit for a few minutes in awkward silence. Finally Mom says, "It's getting late, Son. I'm going to start dinner." She stands and gingerly brushes sand from her hands and the front of her T-shirt.

Not wanting to let go of her reassurance, I also rise and say, "I'll help with dinner."

Mom gently touches my arm and says, "I would rather you go find your father and talk to him. The longer you wait, the harder it will be. You're running out of time."

I nod again and watch Mom turn toward the house. I follow her into the kitchen where I grab a couple of beers from the 'fridge.

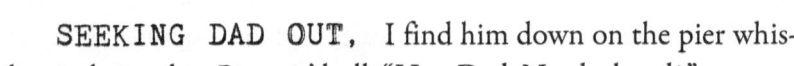

SEEKING DAD OUT, I find him down on the pier whistling as he washes *Pizzazz'* hull. "Hey, Dad. Need a hand?"

"Cam, come on down. I'm almost finished here," Dad says, as he swipes a soapy sponge across the name *Pizzazz,* painted in marine blue script on the white hull of the yacht.

"How 'bout a beer?" I ask and hold up the two bottles of *Millers* as I join him at the end of the dock.

"You may have just saved my life," Dad jokes as he tosses the sponge into a pail of sudsy water and wipes his forearm across his forehead, soaking up the sweat with his shirtsleeve.

I plop down on the wooden planks and dangle my legs over the edge of the pier. Dad soon joins me.

Dad takes the bottle I hand him and holds the coolness to his forehead. "Man, that feels good." After a few moments, he says "You've been pensive the last few days, Cam. Is there something on your mind?"

I'm not surprised at Dad's perceptiveness. Growing up, I thought he was clairvoyant judging from the way he could always see through me. I didn't get away with much and if I did, it was probably because Dad didn't make it an issue. One of his mantras was, "Choose your battles wisely."

I take a swig from the bottle before I begin. "Dad," I say, "although I admire you and what you've done in your chosen profession, I find that I'm being pulled a different direction... I want to write."

I'm amazed at Dad's reaction, he doesn't flinch. I watch him slightly nod his head before taking a pull from the beer bottle. I take a deep breath and encouraged somewhat, I rush on telling him about the internship.

At the end of my dissertation, Dad says, "You are your mother's son—not that there's anything wrong with that." After a few moments, Dad reaches over and tousles my hair. "I'm proud of you, Cam. If that's what you want to do, you have my blessing." Then, after draining the last of his beer, he rises, "Come on, Grisham wanna-be, Mom probably has dinner waiting."

I stand, and grabbing the pail, I walk alongside Dad back to the house. *Parents are amazing creatures! For years they don't know a damn thing then, all of a sudden, they possess the wisdom of Solomon. Go figure!*

PLOT YOUR COURSE

S till steaming, Ashland Prescott sat in his home office reflecting on the incident that occurred the previous evening at a book signing. The event was sponsored by a local bookstore, *Shahrazad Books*, where his current bestseller, *Spellbound,* was being promoted.

Being a narcissist, Prescott had an inflated sense of self-importance. His insecurities had manifested themselves into a deep need for admiration, especially female. Over the years, he had honed his womanizing skills and had become extremely adept at charming women who unwittingly wandered into the crosshairs of his radar. Prescott's thick white hair, Pepsodent smile and perpetual all-over tan, coupled with gushing compliments and his patented 'where have you been all of my life' gaze, usually did the trick and the female *victims* fell at his feet.

Prescott's cold and calculating nature allowed him to discard women like yesterday's newspaper with little or no thought as to how his insensitivity affected the women he left in his wake. He didn't hesitate to start a new relationship before ending the current one. Unfortunately, or perhaps fortunately for the women, his affections seldom lasted more than a few months before Prescott was on the hunt again. Morals and scruples were something that applied to others, certainly not him. Being the only celebrity in town, Prescott was fair game and his philandering delighted the local gossip mongers who never seemed to run out of juicy tidbits.

DURING THE COURSE of the book signing the evening before, one especially attractive woman approached the author's table holding a copy of *Spellbound*. Prescott took special interest in her as she stepped forward. Exposing a generous amount of cleavage, the woman leaned across the table and looking directly into Prescott's eyes, said in a hushed tone, "Your novel was pretty good... that is, up to the murder scene."

"Oh?" Prescott was, of course, taken aback and appeared to be perplexed. His egotistical nature contributed to his fragile self-esteem making him vulnerable even to the slightest censure. Not accustomed to either rejection or criticism, especially from women, he reared back in his chair, folded his arms across his chest and asked, "And how's that?"

The woman straightened to her full height before replying, "Well, I don't want to appear to be rude, but I found the murder scene totally unbelievable. That more or less ruined the rest of the story for me. I couldn't even finish the book."

"I see." Prescott said, apparently abashed that a mere novice would dare critique his writing. Attempting to control his anger, he tapped his pen against the tabletop as he looked around, obviously trying to ascertain if the others standing in line waiting for an autograph had overheard their conversation. Looking back at the woman, he smiled and extended his hand toward the book she was still clutching, "Since we don't give refunds, do you want an autograph?" he joked.

The woman stepped back and slapped the novel down on the table, harshly saying, "You needn't bother, it's not worth signing." She then abruptly turned and walked away. Prescott's face reddened, from rage or embarrassment or both. He contemptuously kept the woman in his gaze as she stalked from the store.

The gentleman next in line apparently overheard the exchange. He, too, watched the woman storm out of the store. Then avoiding eye contact with Prescott, he turned his copy of *Spellbound* over in his hands a couple of times, looking as though he were trying to make a decision. After a few moments, the man stepped out of line and replaced the novel on the bookstore's display shelf, and left. Prescott squirmed as he looked at the other customers still lined up behind the man who had just departed. Obviously, the remaining fans hadn't overheard the woman's remarks because no one else moved to leave. Those still in line appeared eager to get their books signed.

When the last copy had been autographed, Prescott reached across the table and picked up the book the woman had left and roughly paged through it. About midway he found a business card she had apparently been using as a bookmark. It was placed in the chapter depicting the murder scene she had complained about.

SINCE CHILDHOOD, PRESCOTT'S egotistical nature dictated that he retaliate whenever he perceived someone had wronged him. Now sitting in his home office, he seethed, exploring ideas on how to even the score with the bitch that had the nerve to criticize him. He absent-mindedly turned the business card he found in the novel over in his hands several times, inspecting the front and back.

The elaborate engraving on the front of the card identified the woman whom Prescott thought to be the offender as Lisette Kingston, Vice President of Monroe Investments. Prescott knew Monroe Investments to be a small exclusive entity that offered their clients advice on how to survive in today's volatile stock market. The back of the business card had been stamped with Kingston's private phone number and email address. Prescott used the reverse telephone directory to locate the address that corresponded with the telephone number—817 Pelican Way, Coral Cove, FL.

THE FOLLOWING DAY Prescott was up earlier than usual. He had Googled the address and ascertained that it was located in Coral Heights, an area where the estates started in the million- dollar range. His intention was to surveil the address and hoped, if he arrived early enough, to catch a glimpse of the occupant, perhaps leaving for work.

Driving slowly through the estates, Prescott suddenly noticed a garage door begin to rise. Upon closer inspection he observed the house number on the brick column which housed the mailbox identifying the property as 817 Pelican Way. *What luck!* Trying to appear inconspicuous, Prescott pulled to the curb before reaching the cul-de-sac where the target mansion was situated and slouched down in the driver's seat.

The female driver of the late model Lexus looked back over her shoulder as she maneuvered out of the garage onto the street. When she did so, Prescott was able to get a good look at her face; it was the same woman who insulted him at the book signing. Now, having positively identified his prey, Prescott returned home and proceeded with his daily routine.

PRESCOTT LIVED ALONE and his beachfront home was far from his nearest neighbor. Eight years before, his home had been broken into and vandalized and it was then he determined he needed a guard dog. Prescott invested some time researching various breeds of canines before visiting the local kennel.

Now standing outside the cage housing an undernourished Doberman pup, Prescott remembered from his research that the Doberman breed's guarding skills also included the capability of recognizing and responding to threats. The article went on to say that "Dobie's were good companions and fiercely loyal to their masters." *Fiercely loyal to their masters, I like that.*

Prescott didn't hesitate. Upon seeing the scrawny, shaking, sad little pup, he pointed and said to the attendant, "I want that one."

After completing the paperwork, Prescott took the shivering pooch in his arms and as he carried it away from the shelter, he whispered in the dog's ear, "Well, Goliath, I think this is the beginning of a beautiful friendship."

PRESCOTT WAS RELENTLESS in Goliath's training. Each morning, Goliath raced to the patio when Prescott called to him. The dog instinctively knew it was time for their daily five-mile run. When Prescott patted the dog's head and pointed up the beach, Goliath understood that was the command to "Go!" and, like a streak of lightening, Goliath would take the lead. He would occasionally circle back to check on Prescott and after ensuring Prescott was coming along, Goliath would charge ahead merrily splashing through the tide as it ebbed its way back out to sea.

Normally at the end of their run, Prescott would spend some time playing *Frisbee* with Goliath. However, not so today. Prescott had plans to formulate and had no time for folly.

After showering and donning a T-shirt and chinos, Prescott blended himself a breakfast shake and retired to his home office.

His focus was on how to commit murder and get away with it. *I'll show her. My next murder scene will be 'picture perfect.' Too bad she won't be alive to appreciate it.*

WEIGH ANCHOR

D ad has an early showing of a three-million-dollar estate so we
say our farewells before he leaves for his office.

"You take care, Cam. Keep in touch, you know how your
mother worries."

"After twenty-five years, you better believe I do, and I will keep
in touch," I say as I zip my duffels closed.

Dad stands in my bedroom doorway looking forlorn. I walk
over and reach up and tousle his hair the way he used to tousle mine.
We both laugh at the switching of roles.

"I know you'll do fine. The internship will probably be fun as
well as educational," Dad says.

"I'm really looking forward to it, Dad. Not every aspiring
author gets a chance like this." I pause and look around my room.
"Guess I have everything I need..."

"Except this," Dad says and hands me a small gift-wrapped
package.

"Hey, what's this?" I ask.

"Open it and find out, Goofy," Dad teases.

I excitedly rip the paper from the box and when I lift the lid, I'm overcome with emotion. Dad presented me with a Maui diver's watch.

"Dad...I don't know what to say."

"'Thank you' suffices very nicely."

"Yes, thank you. But that seems inadequate compared to the gift." I put the watch on; Dad had already set it. Still gazing at the watch, I say, "I've always wanted a Maui..."

"I know," Dad replies and looks at his watch. "I'd better get going. Don't wanna blow this deal...need the commission to pay for that Maui," Dad jokes as he points to my watch. He turns to walk away, then turns back, "I love you, Son."

Tears threaten to diminish my manhood as I reply, "And I love you, too, Dad."

WHEN I LEFT school for winter break, I vacated my room at the Sigma Chi frat house knowing I wouldn't be returning to live on campus. Thus, I'm able to go directly to my mentor's home in Coral Cove.

After I received Prescott's acceptance of my internship application, we spoke several times on the phone. We coordinated my date of arrival and since that time, I haven't had much contact with him.

When I arrive in Coral Cove, I call him on my cellphone. "Mr. Prescott, this is Cameron Donovan."

"Who?"

"Cameron Donovan—remember, WYU's internship program. You volunteered to mentor me..."

"Oh, yes, of course. I just didn't recognize your name at first."

"That's okay." Then, after a slight awkward pause, I add, "Ahh, the semester is starting Monday and I was wondering if..."

"Of course, say no more. I've been expecting you and if you're ready, you may come as soon as today."

"That's perfect. I'm here in Coral Cove and can be there in fifteen minutes. I just punched in your address on GPS."

"Wonderful." Then he adds, "Since its lunch time, I'll prepare something for us while I wait for you."

WHEN I RING the bell, I can hear a dog bark on the other side of the door and someone scold, "Quiet, Goliath." Then after a brief pause, the door swings open. "Well, come on in." I'm greeted by Ashland Prescott, a dignified, fit, middle-aged man whom I recognize immediately from the photo on the back of his novels.

"Thank you, Mr. Prescott. It's a pleasure to finally meet you," I say as I squeeze through the doorway juggling my two duffels. Once in the foyer, I set the bags down and offer Prescott my hand.

After we perform the obligatory handshake, Prescott says, "Here, let me help you with your bags…" and picks up one of the duffels. "Just follow me and I'll show you to your quarters."

As Prescott chaperones me through the house, I catch glimpses of the living and dining rooms. They are luxurious and most likely put together by a professional decorator. "This is a nice place, a very nice place," I say.

"Why, thank you! Goliath and I like it here."

"Goliath?"

"My Dobie. He's presently hiding. I scolded him for barking when you arrived."

Feeling guilty, I say, "Oh, don't punish him on my account. I love dogs."

"Glad to hear it, Mr. Donovan. However, Goliath is my family and I treat him as such but I also discipline him when he needs it."

"I see." I'm embarrassed and feeling foolish for implying the dog had been reprimanded because of me. I attempt to cover my blunder by changing the subject so I say, "Friends and family call me Cam..."

"Okay, Cam it is. However, I'm still Mr. Prescott."

"Yes, of course." *Good God! I've only been here five minutes and I've already alienated the dog and been scolded by my mentor. Wonder if I made the right decision electing to do this internship?*

When we reach my quarters, Prescott pushes the door open with his foot. He steps in and sets my duffel down just inside the door.

"Here you go, Cam," he says and steps aside allowing me to enter. "I've started lunch so go ahead and wash up. When you're ready, join me on the patio," and he points to the corridor we just traversed that apparently runs the entire length of the mansion. "Down that way and through the sliding glass doors is the kitchen."

I glance in the direction he's pointing and nod.

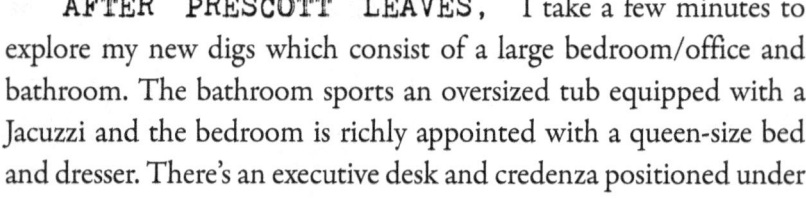

AFTER PRESCOTT LEAVES, I take a few minutes to explore my new digs which consist of a large bedroom/office and bathroom. The bathroom sports an oversized tub equipped with a Jacuzzi and the bedroom is richly appointed with a queen-size bed and dresser. There's an executive desk and credenza positioned under a large window that overlooks the Atlantic. I sit down in the high-backed leather chair and swivel around a couple of times enjoying my new environment. *Perhaps I did make the right decision after all.*

After I wash my hands, I look in the mirror above the sink and notice my hair is a jumble. Quickly searching through the vanity, I find a comb and, after smoothing my hair down, I move to join Prescott. When I step out of the sliding glass doors which separate the kitchen from the patio, I'm instantly struck by a breathtaking panorama of the ocean. Taking a few minutes to admire the view, I suddenly feel something brush against my calves and look down. A large chocolate Doberman, probably Goliath, has obviously completed his "time out" and has joined us. Although his size is intimidating, he seems friendly and even tentative so I reach down and scratch his head; he licks my hand.

"Appears as though Goliath likes you, that's a good sign," Prescott says. He points the butter knife he's holding toward the chair opposite him motioning for me to sit down.

"Yes," I say, "and I like him as well." *Wonder what would happen if Goliath didn't like me? Adiós? This is my last semester and I can't take a chance on messing it up so I resign myself to accept whatever I have to accept in order to complete the course. With that resolve in mind, I maneuver my chair closer to the table and help myself to the spread of cold deli meats, cheese and condiments. When I take the first bite of my sandwich, I suddenly realize how hungry I am and make fast work of the rest.

AFTER LUNCH, I spend the rest of the afternoon getting situated. I hang my clothes in the ample walk-in closet and stash my duffels on the shelves. A computer is already in place on the desk, and logging into my account, I check for email. There are a few messages from classmates and of course, the obligatory message from Mom sending her love and best wishes. And "Oh, by the way, Dad closed the deal on the three-mil estate."

Of course he did. His commission on that deal is probably more than I can expect to earn in the next ten years—guess I get to keep the Maui.

I email a reply,

>Thanks, Mom, for your love and best wishes. Congrats to Dad on closing the deal. Knew he would.
>
>So far, I like it here. My surroundings are very pleasant. After spending almost six years at the U in

Ft. Lauderdale, I find Coral Cove, which is only 25 miles from the U, a pleasant reprieve from the hustle and bustle of the bigger city.

Prescott has a spectacular yacht, Best Seller IV. In case you haven't guessed, the IV indicates the four novels he has had on the New York Times Bestseller list. I can see it from the window in my quarters as he keeps it moored at his pier. It's a nice craft but, of course, Pizzazz is, and will always be, my favorite. Prescott encourages me to take his yacht out whenever I want.

Prescott also has a Doberman named Goliath. Great dog, we've bonded—I think.

More later. Love to you and Dad,
Cam

Just as I push the send key, Prescott taps on my door. When I open it, I see Prescott and Goliath standing there. "Cam, I'm going to town to do some shopping. Would you like to accompany me? I'll show you around."

"Yes, I'd like that," I say, and step out into the corridor. "I'm ready whenever you are."

On our trek to the downtown area, I ride shotgun and Goliath romps around in the back seat of the Range Rover. Prescott, acting much like a tour guide, appears to be content and enjoying showing me the places of interest. On the way home, he takes me on a side tour of an upscale part of town and drives very slowly down an avenue named Pelican Way. I thought it was an odd thing to do. However, I didn't dwell on it. My thought was that he was showing off some of the exclusive property in and around Coral Cove.

TRUE COLORS

The next morning I'm awakened by scratching on my door. *Goliath?* I look at the clock on the night table, 6:15. I groan as I grudgingly toss the sheets back and stagger across the room. When I open the door, Goliath rushes in eagerly wagging his tail.

"Well, good morning to you, too," I say and rub his head. I avail myself of the bathroom facilities while Goliath patiently sits and waits. Just as I pull on a pair of khaki shorts, I hear Prescott shout, "GOLIATH! Come on boy."

Goliath stands and starts for the door, he turns back and approaches me and then turns toward the door again all the while gingerly wagging his tail. I get the message; he wants me to come with him.

"Well, if it makes you happy..." I say and Goliath leads me to a spot on the beach where Prescott is now stretching, apparently warming up for a run.

Prescott looks surprised when he sees me approaching with his dog. He smiles and says, "Looks like Goliath invited you to join us on our daily run." He then looks out across the Atlantic where the sun has just cleared the horizon transforming the clouds to various shades of pink as it journeys skyward. "You up to five miles?" he asks, and squints back at me.

By the tone of his voice and the look on his face, I translate that to be a challenge so I say, "You bet!"

Prescott pauses a moment and looks as though he's sizing me up. He then reaches down and rubs Goliath's head and pointing up the beach, he gives the command, "Go!"

I'm caught off guard as Goliath and Prescott take off simultaneously. *So he is challenging me. Okay then, game on!* It doesn't take me long to close the gap. I could run circles around the older man, but remembering Mom cautioning me more than once that "Discretion is the better part of valor," I choose to adhere to Mom's sage advice. Besides, showing off would just widen the abyss that seems to be forming between me and my mentor. I back off and let him win.

At the end of our run, Prescott slaps me on the shoulder and, still panting, says, "You're in pretty good shape."

I take the cue and respond, "And so are you."

Wiping the sweat from his forehead with his shirt tail, Prescott replies, "Not too bad for an old codger." Then he says, "Go on and shower and meet me in the kitchen. After breakfast, we'll get started on the novel."

At last! I'm eager to commence with the writing. After all, that's what I'm here for. I nod and turn toward the house. As I do so, I sense Prescott burning holes in my back with his gaze; Goliath has fallen in beside *me*. It appears that I have another dilemma that is not so easily resolved. How do I discourage Goliath as he seems to prefer me to Prescott? If I alienate the dog, I incur Prescott's wrath; if I don't, I will still incur Prescott's wrath. Damned if I do and damned if I don't!

PRESCOTT IS SLICING a melon onto a platter and looks up when I enter the kitchen with Goliath at my heels. Prescott appears to be oblivious to what now seems to be my constant companion and I do not detect any reaction from him. He has laid out one place setting on the counter accompanied by milk, orange juice and several boxes of cereal.

Goliath rounds the counter to where Prescott is standing obviously looking for a handout. Prescott ignores him and says to me, "We have a variety of healthy cereals to choose from," and he points with the knife to the collection on the counter. He holds up a tall glass containing a mysterious green concoction and says, "I usually blend myself a smoothie for breakfast."

"H-m-m-m, looks...healthy," I say, "However, I grew up on cereal so I think I'll just have a bowl of flakes."

Prescott sits down on the opposite side of the L-shaped counter that separates the kitchen from the small dining area and begins to thumb through the daily newspaper. He has basically ignored me and we finish breakfast in virtual silence. When I rise and start to clear the dishes, Prescott says, "Leave them. Marcella comes today and she'll do a thorough cleaning, including your laundry. Just drop your soiled clothes off in the utility room."

I hadn't realized the housekeeper also did the laundry so I respond, "That's great. I could get spoiled..."

"Don't worry, I have plenty to keep you busy," Prescott says in a less than jovial tone.

I stand and move to leave, "Since I didn't know Marcella did the laundry, I need to get my dirty duds to the utility room *post haste...*"

"Of course. You go ahead and I'll meet you in my office in a few minutes. I'm going out onto the patio and make a couple of phone calls."

As soon as Prescott leaves, I rush to my quarters to gather my clothes and get my hamper to the laundry room before Marcella arrives. After I deposit my hamper, I head for Prescott's office. I'm concerned Prescott maybe has finished making his calls and is waiting for me and I don't want to incur his disfavor any more than I already have. However, much to my relief, when I arrive I find he's not there yet. Intrigued by Prescott's surroundings, I'm curious as to how an author of his caliber conducts research so I begin to browse, taking it all in. When I move around to the back of Prescott's desk, I notice a business card lying on the floor by his chair. As soon as I pick it up, I hear Prescott's footsteps coming down the hall so I hurriedly jam the card in my pants pocket and round the desk back to the front side. I don't want him to catch me snooping.

When Prescott enters, he raises his brows and suspiciously looks around. He saunters in and positions himself in his chair behind his desk. Then in a stern voice, he says, "Cam, for future reference, I would appreciate it if you don't enter my office if I'm not here."

I'm nervous anyway at almost being caught snooping and respond, "Ah, sure. I didn't mean..."

"It's all right," he says, as he holds up a hand to silence me. Then pointing to a stack of books on his desk, he continues, "I've been doing some research and to date, I have a prologue and two chapters written."

He motions for me to sit in one of the two matching side chairs opposite the desk and pulls a yellow legal notepad from a desk drawer and hands it to me. "Only on rare occasions do I dictate, Cam. I now prefer to write," then he chuckles and adds, "That way, I can see what I'm saying."

I laugh at his little joke although I didn't think it was all that funny. I accept the notepad and look it over. I'm impressed with the quality of his cursive writing and say so. "You have very legible handwriting. I don't think I'll have any trouble trans..."

"Good." He cuts me off midsentence and I'm developing a complex at not being allowed to finish my thoughts before he shuts me down. "I've set you up with all the tools you'll need to prepare my manuscript. You'll notice that I number and date the pages on the upper left hand side. That helps keep me and my transcriber on track." After a brief pause, he continues, "I do a lot of pacing and I'm pretty noisy when I page through research manuals. It's just better if we work in separate rooms."

"Sure, I agree. I like it quiet when I'm concentrating."

Prescott nods and then says, "Your predecessor left you a template on the computer showing exactly how the manuscript is laid out. She titled it *Initial Setup*."

"That's wonderful," I breathe a sigh of relief. If Prescott's computer skills are as poor as he claims, I was dreading the thought of him training me.

"Excellent," he says. "I'll be here all morning. Please do not hesitate to ask questions if need be."

Prescott then looks down and begins to shuffle through some paperwork on his desk. I tarry for a few moments, then realizing I'd been dismissed, I rise to leave. As soon as I open the office door, Goliath, who had been patiently waiting in the corridor, stands and eagerly thumps his tail against my calves. I glance back but it appears that Prescott is oblivious to Goliath's presence. He's still absorbed with the cluster of papers on his desk. I step out into the hallway and tugging Goliath's collar, point toward Prescott and urge the dog towards him, hoping he will join his master.

Stubborn beast that he is, Goliath stands his ground. He prances about, apparently urging *me* to join him. He butts up against my legs, runs forward a few paces and then back to where I'm standing. Not wanting to call too much attention to the predicament, I close Prescott's office door and turn toward my quarters with Goliath running ahead of me.

JUDITH BLEVINS & CARROLL MULTZ

When we reach my room, I decide not to let Goliath in hoping this rejection will discourage him and cause him to wander off. It doesn't. He languishes in the corridor whining and occasionally scratching at the door. *Not good!* I finally cave and let him in. When I do, he moseys over and curls up under my desk. I playfully nudge him with my foot and seemingly content, he's soon fast asleep. *Damn dog!*

———————————

I'M IN A quandary. Although nothing has been said, I sense that Prescott is resentful of the situation. I sit at my desk and mentally examine scenarios on how to discourage the dog. After a few minutes of careful reflection, I come up with nothing that wouldn't alienate both Goliath and Prescott.

I finally give up and engage my computer. I automatically check my email. There's scant renderings from friends and a message from Mom. I open it first; it reads:

Good morning, Son.

Unfortunately, I have some bad news. Yesterday, Dad slipped in some water on Pizzazz' deck and sprained his right ankle. He'll be on crutches for a few weeks, but you know Dad, he's doggedly determined not to let an "insignificant injury" keep him down. We'll see how brave he is when the pain meds wear off!

Other than Dad's misfortune, we're doing as well as can be expected. Dad's colleagues sent him a lovely "get well soon" gardenia bush. Dad's favorite, as you well know. It's in full bloom and smells delightful.

How's life treating you in Coral Cove? We miss you terribly and love hearing from you,

Love from both me and Dad,
Mom

I respond immediately to Mom's email.

Thanks, Mom, for the info on Dad.

> *Today we start Prescott's new novel. However, if you need me, of course I'll come home to help out. I think, under the circumstances, I can get away for a week or so. In fact, that may be a blessing considering I have a situation here I don't know how to cope with. Prescott's Doberman, Goliath, seems to prefer me to his master. I sense Prescott is resentful although he hasn't said anything.*

> *If I leave for a while, perhaps Goliath will think I've deserted him and reverse his loyalty. What do you think?*

As always,
Your loving son, Cam.

After sending Mom my reply, I check the PC for the document titled *Initial Setup* left by my predecessor, Nikki Palmer. Nikki stored it on the computer's desktop making it easy to find. I open the document and upon inspection, I determine Nikki is very efficient; her instructions are detailed and easy to follow.

Following Nikki's outline, I enter the information required by publishers on the first pages of the novel and then I turn my attention to the handwritten pages Prescott gave me this morning. His preliminary title is *Beguiled*. However, Prescott explained to me that sometimes, as the novel unfolds, he changes the title, tailoring it to better fit the story. I'm intrigued by the plot he has laid out and speed along with the transcription of the prologue and first two chapters eagerly looking forward to the succeeding chapters. His style of writing keeps the reader hungry for "what's next."

The morning whizzes by and before I know it, Prescott is at my door announcing that lunch is ready. Goliath, when he hears Prescott's voice, stands and stretches. He ambles to the door, looks back and waits for me to come open it. Before I can get there, Prescott has the door open and Goliath squeezes out into the corridor.

"There you are!" Prescott says. I watch the dog lick Prescott's hand and then dash for his doggie door, apparently in a rush to relieve himself. Prescott watches Goliath leave and then turns his attention to me, "How's the transcribing coming?" he asks as he looks over my shoulder toward the computer.

"Just great." Then, I, too, look back at my desk. "I'm already into it and can't wait for the next chapters." I pause, then say in jest, "Can you write a little faster?"

Prescott smiles at the compliment. "Come on. We're having leftovers from yesterday's lunch."

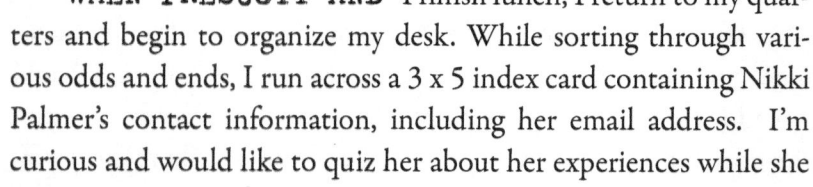

WHEN PRESCOTT AND I finish lunch, I return to my quarters and begin to organize my desk. While sorting through various odds and ends, I run across a 3 x 5 index card containing Nikki Palmer's contact information, including her email address. I'm curious and would like to quiz her about her experiences while she was Prescott's transcriber so I decide to email her. When I open my email, I see I have a reply from Mom, so I read it before composing my message to Nikki.

> *Cam,*
>
> *We are doing well and your presence here, although welcome, wouldn't make a difference. Dad agrees with me. You need to stay there and not take a chance on losing your internship.*
>
> *As far as your dog dilemma is concerned, leaving isn't the answer. You know the old adage, absence*

makes the heart grow fonder? Well, I'm afraid it's even more pronounced where pets are concerned. There are sprays available but in your situation, I wouldn't recommend that you do that. The dog may just be infatuated with you because you're new to his environment—give it time.

Keep us posted.

Love,
Mom

Mom has always given me sage advice and after careful consideration, I agree with her reasoning.

AS I WAIT for Prescott to give me more of the manuscript to transcribe, I can't help but notice that Goliath hasn't come by my room wanting in. *Maybe Prescott locked him out of the house. But still something doesn't feel right...* After a while, I put my concern behind me and prepare an email to Nikki. Earlier, Prescott described her to me as an intelligent, serious college student who is a perfectionist.

"She didn't talk much so I know little about her personal life," Prescott had said. "She took a selfie with Goliath before she left and printed me a copy. I appended it to the refrigerator door. Think it's still there."

I then remembered seeing the photo of an extremely attractive blond with a killer figure kneeling with one arm around Goliath's neck. I thought it was a relative or friend of Prescott.

My email to Nikki Palmer reads:

Hello, Nikki.

My name is Cameron Donovan, better known as "Cam." I'm a graduate student at WYU and am participating in the internship program offered to last-semester journalism students by the U. Your former employer, Ashland Prescott, is mentoring me as I aspire to write the great American novel.

I want to compliment and thank you for having the foresight to put the initial setup template on the computer. It's made my life much easier. I would like to meet you and treat you to lunch in town sometime soon. If you agree, shoot me back a reply letting me know when and where.

Regards,

Cam

P.S. I'm sure if Goliath could talk he'd ask me to send you greetings, so I'll do it anyway. 'Bark-bark.'

I didn't have to wait long for a reply from Nikki. Her return email reads:

Cam,

I would be happy to have lunch with you. I'm willing to do whatever it takes to help you along with the great American novel. Can you meet me at the Blue Dolphin on Saturday at noon? Please confirm.

Nikki

P.S. Your bark-bark greeting from Goliath sealed the deal! I'm extremely fond of that pest!

I, of course, fired a reply back to Nikki confirming that I would meet her on Saturday. Things are looking up.

ACCORDING TO PRESCOTT, The *Blue Dolphin* is the place where the locals go for seafood. I remember him pointing it out when he took me on the tour of downtown a few days ago.

I locate my target and step into the cool, dim entrance of the quaint little restaurant. After being out in the bright sunlight, I'm suddenly blinded by the dim interior and I squint as I look around. After a few moments, my vision returns to normal and I spot Nikki whom I recognize from the photo sitting at the bar. When I approach, she looks up.

"Cam?"

"Yes," I extend my hand in greeting. "Thank you for accepting my invitation..."

"Well, thank you for the invite," Nikki replies and turns to retrieve her shoulder bag from the barstool next to her. She stands and asks, "Where would you like to sit?"

"Oh, I don't know," I say, "Since I'm the new kid on the block, you pick."

She takes me by the hand and leads me to a booth away from the noisy bar. "I like to sit in booths," she says. "It's quieter and more private."

As soon as we are situated, a waitress appears with water and menus and asks if we would like something from the bar. I look at Nikki.

Nikki nods, "Yes, I'd like a Corona with a wedge."

"Sounds good, I'll have the same."

I pick up the menu and as soon as the waitress leaves, I ask, "Since this is my first visit to the *Blue Dolphin,* what do you suggest?"

Nikki reaches over and points to an item featured in the middle of the menu. "My favorite," she says.

Her favorite is listed as Fish and Chips. That instantly appeals to me. "Okay then, I'll take your word for it."

When the waitress returns with our beer, I order the fish and chips for us both.

"It'll be right up, sir," the waitress says and turns toward the kitchen.

Nikki watches the waitress retreat, then asks, "So, Cam, how do you like working for Prescott?"

I have to smile when it occurs to me that she also refers to him as *Prescott*. Mimicking Prescott, I say, "That's Mr. Prescott to you!"

Nikki's face breaks into a wide grin. "Touché," she says.

I tilt my bottle her direction in salute. "To answer your question, so far so good. However, I've just barely started."

"Um-hum."

Wonder what that means. "How long did you work with him?" I ask.

"M-m-m-m, let's see, I guess about a year over the span of two semesters. The internship program wasn't available to me since I'm not a journalism major. But, because he posted an ad for a typist in the *Touchstone*, I assumed he must not have had anyone requesting to mentor with him the semesters I did his typing."

"I see." I squeeze the lime into the beer bottle and take a swig. Not wanting to vilify my mentor by revealing my true feelings, I say, "I like his style of writing and I already feel like I'm learning a technique."

Nikki nods. "By the way, how's Goliath?" she asks.

He's doing well. But, he should have been named *Velcro*."

Nikki laughs, "You, too? He was my constant companion. I couldn't get away from him and I only spent a few hours a day there. Can't imagine what it's like dealing with him 24/7."

"Know what you mean. However, once he gets his way, he curls up under my desk and goes to sleep so it isn't as bad as you think." Then I add, "Prescott must have locked him out of the house. I haven't seen or heard him all morning long."

Nikki furrows her brow and says, "That's unusual…"

So, I'm not the only one fraught with suspicion. "Yes, it is, considering that Goliath 'is a member of the family.'"

Nikki grins again. *She must have been subjected to the same lecture I received from Prescott.*

We sit in silent reflection for a few moments and before I can ask her what she's thinking, our lunch is served. The steaming platter heaped with batter-dipped, deep-fried cod and French fries smells heavenly and I can hardly wait to dig in. Nikki shakes her napkin out and places it on her lap. She then sloshes a generous amount of catsup over her French fries and malt vinegar over the cod. I follow suit. After all, this is her bailiwick.

After a few moments of gorging myself, I come up for air and ask, "Do you live in Coral Cove?"

"Uh-huh, on the outskirts. In fact, just a few miles from Prescott's, albeit not on the same scale as his place. We live in my father's ancestral cottage which is also located on the ocean front." Nikki pauses briefly before adding, "Dad was offered a virtual fortune for the property by a hotel chain but he chose not to sell. I was only ten at the time but I still have a vivid recollection of standing there watching Dad jab his finger into the realtor's chest shouting, 'Tis me family home and link to me past. I'll not have it desecrated by a hotel magnate!'" Nikki then twists her features into a scowl, apparently mimicking the look on her father's face.

"Good man!" I retort. Then having noticed that Nikki hasn't mentioned her mother, I ask, "Does your mother..."

"She died when I was a baby." Nikki sets her fork down on her platter before continuing, "I don't have any memory of her other than what Dad tells me." A melancholy smile graces Nikki's face when she says, "He told me my mother nicknamed me *Snow White* because 'I was her little princess.'"

"I apologize, I didn't mean to pry."

"You're not prying. It's just that I never think of mentioning my mother since I never had a chance to know her."

I nod, then say, "You live that close to Prescott's?"

"Yep. During the time I worked for him, I'd jog the three miles to his place and then jog home again at the end of my work day." She looks down at her platter and adds, "That's the reason I can eat like this and not gain weight."

"Looks like it's working," I say. Then I instantly recognize my comment may have been inappropriate so I rush on to cover my blunder, "By golly, we, that is Prescott, Goliath and me, run five miles a day. We probably turn just a half-mile before we get to your house."

"I know. I've occasionally seen you running with Prescott and Goliath." She pauses, "Sometimes I take a morning swim in the Atlantic, that's how I managed to spot the two of you. Do you like to swim?" she asks.

"Ahh, I much prefer diving."

"I've never dived. Maybe you could teach me?"

I cringe when I think about getting into the water over my head remembering the day I almost drowned. However, I manage to say, "Sure, I'd like that."

WHEN WE LEAVE the *Blue Dolphin*, I walk Nikki to her car. "Thanks, Cam, lunch was great and I enjoyed meeting you."

"Likewise. We'll have to do it again...soon."

Nikki nods. Then she says as she unlocks her car door, "I'm curious about Goliath, let me know when he shows up... please."

"You bet. I, too, am getting a little worried. You don't think Prescott would..." I stop short of putting my thought into words.

"Oh, heavens no! He seems to be devoted to Goliath and I really don't think he would harm him." I watch Nikki's face darken. *Wonder what she's thinking? Prescott didn't show any resentment when Goliath clung to me, but...who knows? I wonder if I should ask him if he knows what happened to Goliath. Maybe not; I could be next on the hit list!*

As Nikki opens her car door and slips onto the driver's seat, I suddenly realize that I hate parting with her. Other than a few scattered emails from college buddies, I've had no outside contact with my contemporaries. Besides, I like her company and the camaraderie we share—not to mention her other attributes.

Partly for the company and partly out of curiosity, I ask, "Other than the proper way to address Prescott and careful not to alienate Goliath's affection, do you have any other helpful hints?"

Nikki retrieves several items from the passenger seat and tosses them onto the backseat. She then motions for me to climb in. "I'm not paranoid," she says, "I just thought you would be more comfortable sitting down."

"I knew I was in for a lecture whenever my parents or the principal ordered me to be seated," I say.

"It's better than being told to 'stand in the corner,'" Nikki replies. We both laugh and I round the car and climb inside.

"Prescott is not susceptible to suggestions," Nikki begins. "He perceives suggestions as criticism. I learned that early on."

"I gathered that," I reply, welcoming the heads-up. "What about the grammatical errors?"

"Prescott made it plain the day I started that my job description was one of transcription, not editing. Not transcribing his notes *verbatim,* and I mean *verbatim,* is nothing short of a mortal sin—at least as far as he is concerned. You will not last long if you transgress."

"What about spelling errors?"

"He has chided me for misspelled words in his manuscripts. Apparently, he considers them my miscues and not his. My advice is to make sure your corrections are not alternate spellings and are one hundred percent accurate."

"I notice some of his paragraphs are lengthy. I assume to suggest paragraph breaks would be the kiss of death."

"Every author, and Prescott is no exception, justifies everything by calling it 'writer's style'. He emphasizes that every writer 'of any worth' has his or her own particular style. One of the examples he is fond of using is that of an author he met while attending a conference at the United States Air Force Academy in Colorado Springs, Colorado, whose style was omitting punctuation. That was acceptable because that was her style." Nikki raises her eyebrows, glancing my direction.

"I remember reading one of her novels in our writing class at the U. As I recall it was *The Last Five Dollar Baby*. Everyone agreed that although it defied all the rules, it was effective."

"My point is that there are two ways to write— according to Prescott—his way and the wrong way."

"Who's to argue with a bestselling author?" I offer. "You raise the flag and if everyone salutes, you have a consensus."

"Has Prescott given you the plagiarism lecture yet?" Nikki asks.

"Is he paranoid about that?" I ask.

"He keeps his manuscripts and notes under lock and key and reveals neither the title nor the contents until he has the copyright. Since titles to books are non-copyrightable, he is always worried other writers may dilute his works by using the same or a similar title."

"Yep," I say, as I lean back and hook my elbow out of the open car window. "Before I began my internship, Prescott had me sign a confidentiality agreement with regard to the manuscripts I work on and any trade secrets I learn during my association with him. He said it was a form recommended by his attorney."

"That's Prescott," Nikki says. He considers writing a craft as much as an art form."

THE NEXT WEEK, as Marcella is sorting the laundry, she finds Kingston's business card along with some coins and paperclips crammed in the new-comer's jean's pockets. She sets them aside and will later put them in the new-comer's in-basket in his quarters. This protocol was established some time ago when Marcella first started housekeeping for Prescott. She washed a pen in the pocket of one of Prescott's shirts, ruining the shirt. Since then, she religiously checks all pockets before washing the clothes and if she finds anything, she places the items in Prescott's, or whoever's, in-basket.

PRESCOTT HAD BEEN writing the scene in his new novel that led up to the murder and when he finished the chapter, he took the pages to Cam's room. Since Cam hadn't returned from town yet, Prescott moved to put the pages in Cam's in-basket. As he did so, he noticed Lisette Kingston's crumpled business card lying in the jumble of coins and other miscellaneous items, apparently placed there by Marcella. Prescott picked up the business card and closely studied it before jamming it into *his* pants pocket. *So, the kid was snooping.*

WHEN I ARRIVE back at Prescott's, I determine by the closed door that he's secluded in his office and not wanting to disturb him, I go directly to my quarters. Checking my in-basket, I find a few new pages to be transcribed and an assortment of coins and other odds and ends which I recognize as clutter from my pants pockets. *Marcella probably left this stuff here for me.* I collect the coins and put them in my pocket and throw the other clutter into a desk drawer.

When I've completed the few pages of transcription Prescott left for me, I take the printed copies to Prescott's office. The door is still closed so I take the printout back to my quarters. I'm lonely and restless and eventually wander out to the patio. I'm hopeful Goliath has returned so I call him. No response! I remove my shoes and walk along the beach in the surf hoping if the dog is near he will see me and join me. No luck!

BY THE TIME I finish my walk, Prescott has emerged from his office and is sitting on the patio. When I approach, he says, "Cam, I have a business meeting in town this evening so you're on your own for dinner. There's some entrées in the freezer—help yourself to whatever you like."

"Okay, thanks, I will," I reply, then add, "I've finished the pages you left: do you have any more of the manuscript ready for me to transcribe?"

"No, not yet...but we're *now* getting to the exciting part," he responds and I notice a strange look cross his face.

After an awkward silence, I say, "I'm sitting on pins and needles. Can you give me a clue as to what happens next?"

Prescott laughs. "My, you are impatient. Sorry, you'll just have to wait. I'm still working it out."

I nod. Then I ask, "Oh, by the way, have you seen Goliath today?"

"No."

"H-m-m-m. Just wondering, neither have I." When I mention Goliath, I notice that strange look cross Prescott's face again.

A COUPLE OF hours after Prescott leaves for his meeting, I rummage through the freezer and select an Italian frozen dinner consisting of a combination of lasagna and spaghetti. It's large enough for two and I consider inviting Nikki to join me. Since I didn't have the presence of mind to get her phone number at lunch today, I take the chance that she may be at her computer. I write:

Hey, Nikki,

I'm home alone. Prescott had an appointment in town this evening. I found a pretty decent looking Italian dinner in the freezer. It's big enough for two; would you like to share it with me? If so, I'll meet you half way so we both get three miles in and can eat the lasagna guilt-free. I'll pop the dinner in the oven before I leave and it should be ready by the time we make it back here.

Cam

I push the send key and sit tapping a pen on my desk top while I wait hoping for a quick response. Within five minutes I get a reply. It reads:

Cam,

Yes! I love Italian almost as much as I love fish and chips. I have some ice cream and cookies which I'll contribute to the dinner. I need to clean up a bit so I'll leave here in 15 minutes or so which should give you time enough to get the dinner in the oven. Meet you half-way.

Nikki

Upon receiving Nikki's reply, I spring into action. I'd already preheated the oven so I place the dinner on the center rack and quickly set the table on the patio. *Wonder if Prescott would mind if we drank a bottle of his wine—who cares!* I'm feeling reckless so I pop the cork on a bottle of white zin to allow it to breathe and set it in a bucket of ice. Satisfied my preparations are acceptable, I sprint down to the surf and begin my trek toward the rendezvous. I soon see that Nikki has closed the gap between us in record time. She covered the distance much quicker than I.

"Are... you the star... of the track team?" I breathlessly manage to pant when we come together.

"Nope, I cheated and left sooner than I anticipated." She then held up a plastic grocery bag, "I brought a suit in case we want to go for a swim after dinner."

I didn't want to admit that I have an aversion to swimming in the ocean which probably goes back to the day I almost drowned. "That's..." I begin, trying to come up with an excuse not to go swimming but she cuts me off midstride.

"Thought you might agree so I didn't waste time cleaning up."

"Un-huh. And here I thought that was a bag of ice cream and cookies..."

"Would you rather it be?" she asks in a salacious tone.

"Not on your life!" I answer. "I'll choose bikinis over cookies every time."

"Well, because you gave the *right* answer, you get both; bikini and cookies."

"What! No ice cream?"

"You're pushing the envelope, Bucko!"

We slowed to a walk and holding hands, we waded barefoot the rest of the distance through the surf as it ebbed along the shore. I had placed a hurricane lamp in the center of the patio table when I set it for dinner and it now beckoned to us from the gloom as we grew closer to the house.

When Nikki saw it, she squeezed my hand and said very softly, "Romantic." I squeezed back.

WHEN WE REACH the patio, we use the garden hose to rinse the sand from our feet. I then point to a chair positioned at the table, and say, "You sit while I fetch dinner. After all, you are my guest."

Before Nikki can protest, I'm already inside sliding the screen door closed. I cross the kitchen to the range leaving a trail of wet footprints in my wake. When I peer into the oven, I find the dinner is piping hot so using oven mitts, I take it out to the patio and set it on the glass top table, then take the chair across from Nikki and pour us each a glass of wine.

I raise my glass and tip it toward Nikki. "Here's to good fortune, good friends, good food and of course, good wine. May your life be filled with an abundance of each."

Nikki clinks her glass against mine and says, "And yours as well."

The frozen dinner is surprisingly good and as we dine, we're wrapped in a delicious warm breeze wafting in from the ocean. The sound of the waves kissing the shore enhance the romantic atmosphere and I notice how lovely Nikki looks as the light of the hurricane candle dances across her face. I can't help staring at her. She's a dichotomy—she tries to put on a 'tomboy' façade but her natural femininity belies her deceit. I'm mesmerized by her and suddenly something stirs inside of me; something I'd never experienced before. *Love?*

I snap back to the present when Nikki asks, "What are you thinking! You have a strange expression on your face."

Damn, are my feelings that transparent? Feeling trapped, I rattle my brain to come up with a plausible reply.

"Oh, ahh, I was just wondering what could have happened to Goliath."

"Un-huh. What do you think?"

"I don't want to think what I'm thinking but..."

"Don't say it! I don't want to think that either."

We sit in silence for a few minutes and I hate myself for putting a damper on the evening by mentioning the dog. I finally say, "Come on, let's get wet!" and I take her hand and pull her to her feet.

She hesitates, "Are you sure you want to..."

"Hell yes! Why, you carried that heavy bikini three miles and it would be a shame to let your labor go to waste."

"Right!"

I point to the house, "You use the guest suite to change and I'll meet you back here in five minutes."

"Five minutes? Impossible! Only Superman can change that fast," she replies and heads for the sliding doors. "Besides, you don't have a phone booth," she shouts back at me as she disappears into the house.

I MUST ADMIT that romping in the surf with Nikki was the highlight of my stay thus far. Her blonde hair was pulled up into a ponytail and she sported a perfect tan; she looked like a Barbie Doll in her bikini, albeit with more meat on her bones.

I chose not to swim but stood chest high in the water and watched as Nikki showed off her skill. Much to my delight, she would occasionally swim up to me and encircle my waist with her legs and wrap her arms around my neck. On one such encounter, she gave me a wet kiss on the lips. That very night, I developed a new appreciation for the taste of saltwater as we frolicked in the tide.

After about thirty minutes of playing in the water, we wrap it up. Back at the house, Nikki showers in the guestroom and I perform a like ritual in my quarters. When she finally appears, I take her hand.

"Come on, you little mermaid, it's late, I'll drive you home. I think we've had enough exercise for one evening."

Nikki blushes and it suddenly occurs to me what she thought I meant by "enough exercise for one evening." It's tempting but I don't want to scare her off by moving too fast so I ignore the possibilities. She slides her arm into mine and rests her head on my shoulder as we walk the short distance from the house to my car. No words are necessary.

When we arrive at Nikki's, she moves close to me and plants a kiss on my cheek. She then quickly slips from the car and runs to her door. Before going inside, she turns and throws me a kiss. When I return it with a kiss of my own, I regret my decision to remain celibate, at least for the time being, and wish this evening wasn't ending. *Yep, if this isn't love, it's a damn close relative.*

ONCE BACK HOME and before I turn in, I send Mom an email:

Hi Mom,

> *Just checking on you and Dad. How's his ankle doing?*
>
> *We're finally making progress and have completed a couple of chapters in Prescott's novel. He's hard to figure; sometimes he's as friendly as can be, other times, forget it. However, this has been an interesting experience and I'm learning from interning with him which makes it worthwhile.*
>
> *Also, I met someone. Her name is Nikki Palmer. She transcribed for Prescott before me. She's an undergrad in her senior year. We seem to have a lot in common.*
>
> *Not only is she smart, she's gorgeous. I know what you're thinking and...you're absolutely right!*
>
> *I think my buddy, Goliath, may have met with an unfortunate end. He's been missing for three days and that's very unlike him. Strangely enough, Prescott doesn't seem to be too concerned about Goliath's disappearance. Like I said, Prescott's hard to figure.*

More later,

Love,
Cam

WALK THE PLANK

Prescott had murder in his heart. He had intensely researched various ways to accomplish his goal. Now that he was ready to implement his scheme, the dilemma was not how but *if* and *when* to strike; there were many options available.

Remembering every tiny detail of the murder, *down to the bitch's last breath*, was paramount to recreating the homicide exactly *and unbelievably* in his current novel. The two things he was unyielding on were, before she died, that she would know it was him, and that she would know why.

As the murder scheme unfolded in his head, Prescott remembered a plot from an old WWII movie he had seen years ago. An assault team was commissioned to eliminate an enemy stronghold. After extensive recon and planning, the attack force put their plan of action, down to the last detail, into rhyme and set it to cadence. Each member of the team memorized the verse and they practiced it in unison several times a day. Nothing was left to chance and the plan worked perfectly.

Knowing how nervous he would be, Prescott decided to use the same principle as the filmmakers. He set his timeline to rhyme and then he, too, mentally rehearsed it several times a day.

Slip inside when she opens the garage,
Position yourself for the sabotage.

Grab the bitch at the kitchen door,
Once inside, shove her to the floor.

Place the tape over her yap,
Before she realizes it's a trap.

Her hands and feet tie in binds,
Quickly close all the blinds.

Make sure she sees the shiny knife.
The one that will end her life.

Ask her if it's still inconceivable,
Or maybe now it's believable.

Remember each and every detail,
As fear makes her face grow pale.

After you complete the crime,
Look around, take your time.

Make sure you've left no clue,
Of anything that would point to you.

PRESCOTT, NOW STANDING in the shadows of the foliage surrounding Kingston's house, secreted himself close to the garage door. The waiting was gnawing at his nerves and he was even considering leaving when, finally, he saw headlights approaching. Through his persistent surveillance, he knew that Kingston opened her garage door about half-way up the block before entering the cul-de-sac where her mansion was situated. He couldn't tell if the oncoming vehicle was his target's because the headlights were so bright. However, when he heard the gears of the overhead door kick in, he knew it was Kingston arriving home. He slumped to a crouch and as soon as the garage door began to rise and there was enough clearance, he ducked under it and hid just inside the kitchen door.

Kingston entered the garage and closed the overhead door. She exited the vehicle, and juggling her purse, opened the kitchen door and stepped inside. Prescott immediately grabbed her and to his surprise, she was stronger than he envisioned. During a brief scuffle, she managed to knock over a canister strewing flour across the counter top and onto the floor. However, despite her desperate struggles, he was able to overcome her and his plan was executed almost flawlessly.

Prescott grabbed Kingston by the hair and lifted her head just far enough off of the floor for her to see the knife he was holding. "Is this murder scene realistic enough for your discernable taste?" he whispered into her ear and then watched recognition form in her eyes an instant before she died. *Mission accomplished!*

AFTER THE MURDER, Prescott carefully looked around the crime scene. He gave a quick thought to cleaning the flour off the counter top and the floor. However, he determined it was not necessary to take the risk of leaving incriminating evidence behind—such as DNA and footprints—so he left it and stealthily slipped out the front entrance setting the lock behind him.

BEYOND THE SEA

When I awake the next morning and go to the kitchen, I don't see Prescott or Goliath. *Maybe Goliath finally showed up and they left early for their morning run.* I pour myself a glass of orange juice and take it out to the patio where I sit trying to clear my head from the wine I consumed the night before. I'm not sure when Prescott arrived home but he wasn't there when I went to bed around midnight.

Before long, the cool morning breeze revives me and I'm beginning to feel human again. It isn't long before Prescott joins me on the patio. He's holding a mug of steaming coffee and has the morning paper tucked under his arm. Taking the chair opposite me, he flips open the paper. When he does so, I read the headline: *CORAL COVE WOMAN FOUND MURDERED IN HER HOME.*

Holding the paper in both of his hands, Prescott gives it a shake to smooth out the middle fold. He adjusts his glasses and reads the article aloud.

> The body of Lisette Kingston, age 46, was discovered by a coworker, Sandra Evans, late last night. Kingston, who had been stabbed several times, was

61

found by Evans lying on her kitchen floor in a pool of blood.

Evans reported to authorities that she and Kingston planned to meet at Choa's Oriental Garden for dinner earlier that evening. When Kingston failed to show, Evans called Kingston's cellphone but Kingston didn't answer. When Evans tried a second time with no answer, she became worried. Evans told authorities that she knew Kingston kept her cellphone with her at all times. Evans said Kingston's commitment to her clients was first and foremost on her list of priorities. Evans also said that, because of the volatile nature of the investment business, Kingston was always available by phone.

When Evans was asked by Coral Cove Detective Blake Corrigan how she gained entry into Kingston's home, Evans explained that, because Kingston lived alone, she gave Evans a key to her house telling her that '...if someday I don't show up for work, come check on me.' Evans reported that when she didn't get a response on the second call, she went to Kingston's home to make sure she was all right and that's when she discovered Kingston's body.

Authorities report that there were no signs of forced entry. All the doors and windows were locked, leading authorities to believe the killer was someone Kingston knew and welcomed into her home. Detective Corrigan said, as far as they could determine at this juncture, robbery did not appear to be the motive. Kingston's purse containing over one hundred dollars in cash was found undisturbed close to her body. A blood covered fish cleaning knife, believed to be the murder weapon, was found at the scene. The ME places the time of death at approximately 7:30 p.m.

When Prescott finishes the article, he looks up from the paper and says, "H-m-m-m, the name of the victim sounds familiar. However, I can't place where I've heard it." Then looking at me, he asks, "Does the name Lisette Kingston sound familiar to you?"

What the hell, I just blew into town. "Nope, I've never heard it before either," I say.

Then with what sounds like relief in his voice, he says, "Wonder who she pissed off?"

I'm stunned at Prescott's insensitivity. I just look at him unable to respond. Prescott seems to be oblivious to my reaction as he stands and tucks the folded paper under his arm.

"Cam, if you like, you can take the day off. I'm going to barricade myself and get some serious writing done today. Today's the day I pen the death scene."

"Thanks, I think I will." Then I watch as he strolls toward his office. *Wonder why he thought I'd recognize the name of the murdered woman?*

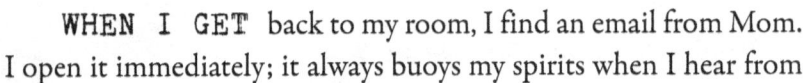

WHEN I GET back to my room, I find an email from Mom. I open it immediately; it always buoys my spirits when I hear from Mom. It reads:

Dear Cam,

*Dad is healing but, of course, not fast enough to suit him. He's turned into Scrooge. Doc says three more weeks on crutches. Dad howled with anguish when he heard that. Be glad you're **not** here. If you were here* *with Dad, you wouldn't restrict your 'sometimes he's as friendly as can be, other times, forget it' comment strictly to Prescott. That could apply to almost anyone...except me, of course.*

We read the newspaper account regarding the homicide in Coral Cove. Pretty gruesome stuff. How far are you from the 'city?' If you detect worry in that comment, you're intuitive. We are, of course, concerned for your welfare. It's our job as parents.

I'm waiting with baited breath for the new novel to be published and especially since you're involved with it, even if only in a peripheral way.

Dad and I are curious about your romantic interest. You were pretty vague regarding Nikki. Smart and gorgeous is a good start but, Mr. Aspiring Novelist, could you be more specific and provide a few more details? We're eager to hear about her.

By the way, has your buddy, Goliath, resurfaced yet? If not, be patient, dogs are good at finding their way home.

Love,
Mom

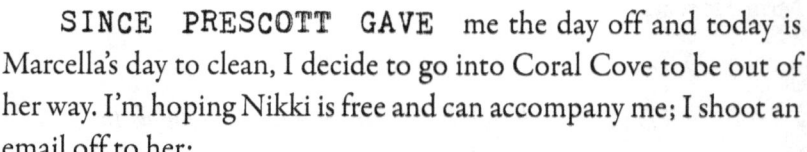

SINCE PRESCOTT GAVE me the day off and today is Marcella's day to clean, I decide to go into Coral Cove to be out of her way. I'm hoping Nikki is free and can accompany me; I shoot an email off to her:

Nikki,

Thanks for such a great time last night. I'm the recipient of another reprieve.

Prescott is hunkering down and gave me the day off. Are you available to go into town and maybe see a movie or do whatever folks do in Coral Cove?

Cam

The girl must spend all of her time at the computer. I receive an instant reply.

Cam, yes, I'd love to. I'll pack a picnic. If 11:30 works, I'll be ready.

Nikki

Nikki was fussing with some flowers along the walkway when I maneuver my Volkswagen Jetta, an early graduation present from my parents, up the winding driveway. When she sees me, she looks up and waves. She sprints into the house and is back a few minutes later carrying a large wicker basket.

Nikki stores the basket on the rear seat and climbs into the passenger seat. "Your invite is a much needed diversion. I've been spending my life at my computer researching and preparing my thesis."

So, that explains why she replies to my emails so quickly.

Nikki continues, "I don't have classes today and after last night I find my usual day off routine pretty boring."

I laugh, "Last night was fun. However, I feel guilty and should explain why I'm not much of a swimmer. I almost drowned when I was ten. Guess that scared the living daylights outta me. Ever since that frightening incident I don't like to get in too deep—in more ways than one."

"Ah-ha," Nikki exclaims. "That explains it—in more ways than one."

I feel my face flush as I pull out of the driveway and head for town. Hoping to divert attention away from my embarrassment, I ask, "What do folks usually do around here during the week?"

"The Cove is pretty laid back," Nikki says as she fastens her seatbelt. "The locals are busy making a buck off the tourists. The tourists are busy trying to negotiate a better deal with the locals. It's a vicious circle."

I nod. "Okay. So, since we're not merchants or tourists, what do we do?"

"I have a special place just outside of town down on the beach. Sometimes, between classes, I go there to study." Nikki pauses then adds, "Wanna see it?"

"Sure, I'd like to go, that is, if I don't have to get wet." I then say, "I have something I want to discuss with you, anyway."

Nikki sits up straighter, looks at me and says, "Now you've aroused my curiosity. Drive faster!"

WHEN WE ARRIVE at Nikki's special place on the beach, we spread a small blanket on the sand and Nikki lays out the lunch she prepared. Once we're settled, she sits cross-legged on the blanket, cocks her head and demands, "WELL?"

I'm in the middle of chewing a bite of sandwich and almost choke at her abruptness. I hold up an index finger indicating for her to give me a moment.

"Unless you speak, and soon, you're going into the drink, the deep end," she scolds.

"I can't help it." I begin to laugh and spew bits of the tuna salad everywhere. Nikki looks disgusted but before long, she, too, is laughing.

Once we regain our composure, I ask, "Did you read the article in this morning's newspaper regarding the murder in Coral Cove?"

"Yes. Why?"

"Well, I was sitting on the patio this morning when Prescott joined me. He had a copy of the *Gazette* and proceeded to read the article out loud to me. When he did so, a strange darkness crossed his face. When he finished reading, he said he thought he had heard Kingston's name but couldn't remember when or where. Then much to my amazement, he asked me if I knew the victim. When I said I didn't, he causally remarked, 'Wonder who she pissed off.'"

"H-m-m-m," Nikki responds. "I don't know how much credence I'd give to his action or inaction to any given circumstance. In case you haven't noticed, authors are a strange breed, and especially him."

"Okay... if you say so." *Wonder if she thinks I'm strange since I aspire to be a writer.*

"Oh, my! You should see the look on your face," Nikki squeals. "You're not included in that last remark since you're not yet an author. The great American novel is yet to be born."

"Whew! That's a relief," I lean back on my elbows and add, "That's not all, Nikki. When I mentioned Goliath's disappearance, once again that darkness jumped into his eyes. I think he knows what happened to Goliath."

Nikki, looking thoughtful as she chewed on a potato chip, finally says, "I agree. I think Prescott couldn't take the rejection and just did away with the source of his irritation." After a few moments of reflection, she asks, "Are you implying he may have had something to do with the Coral Cove murder?"

"No!" I pause, "Well, I don't know. His reaction was certainly strange to say the least." Then I ask, "Did he ever expose a violent side to you during the time you worked for him?"

"H-m-m-m, no, I don't think... Wait! I take that back. There was the time, in fact, just recently when he came home from a book signing at the local bookstore, *Shahrazad Books,* and went into a rage. He banged the front door closed and stormed into his office and slammed his valise down on his desk. He was pacing back and forth, waving his arms around and ranting about some 'damned bitch' and, he said, 'I'll show her.' Goliath was so startled at the outburst that he started barking. Prescott kicked at him but missed. I fear if he had connected, Goliath would have needed to see a vet."

"How long ago did you say that was?" I ask.

"Right before you came on board. I was finishing up my projects anticipating your arrival. That's why I was there so late that night."

"Did you ever feel threatened by him?"

"No. Never. However, when I left, after the scene he created, I was thankful I didn't have to work for him any longer."

There's a lot of speculation tumbling around in my head and I suspect Nikki is experiencing much the same reaction. We abort our conversation for the time being and pack up the picnic remains and store the basket in the Jetta. After we complete the cleanup, I suggest we walk up the beach.

Wading barefoot through the surf, I look over at Nikki; she appears to be solemn and I wonder what she's thinking. I'm surprised when she suddenly grabs my hand and says, "Cam, promise me you'll be careful. Even if Prescott wasn't involved in the Coral Cove incident, anyone that would destroy his pet for revenge has a real mean streak."

"You bet I'll be careful." I squeeze her hand, "After all, we haven't written the great American novel yet."

"We?"

"Yep. Couldn't do it without you and now, I wouldn't even want to."

Nikki rewards me with a kiss on the cheek. I respond by encircling her waist with my arms and pulling her close. Before long we find ourselves cast in the roles of Bert Lancaster and Deborah Kerr reenacting the famous love scene on the beach from the movie *From Here to Eternity.*

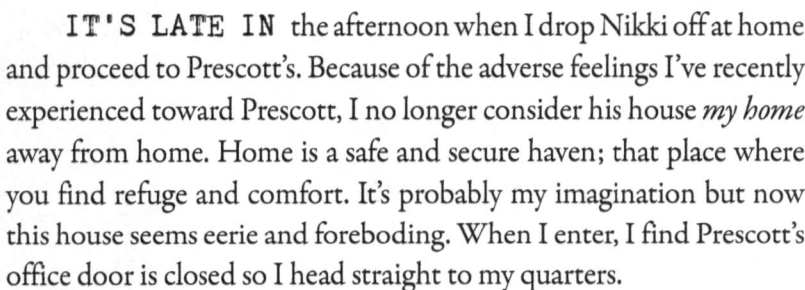

IT'S LATE IN the afternoon when I drop Nikki off at home and proceed to Prescott's. Because of the adverse feelings I've recently experienced toward Prescott, I no longer consider his house *my home* away from home. Home is a safe and secure haven; that place where you find refuge and comfort. It's probably my imagination but now this house seems eerie and foreboding. When I enter, I find Prescott's office door is closed so I head straight to my quarters.

The sand embedded in my skin from the afternoon's romp on the beach with Nikki is beginning to itch so the first thing I do is take a shower. Feeling somewhat refreshed, I wrap a towel around my waist and head for my computer where I check for messages. Nothing. I sit down on the edge of my bed and pull on a pair of clean shorts and a T-shirt. I'm suddenly so exhausted I can barely focus so I lie back on my bed and soon fall into a deep, dreamless sleep.

EARLY THE NEXT morning, I'm awakened when my cell-phone rings. I manage a weak "'Lo."

"Cam, its Mom."

Now I'm wide awake and sit straight up in bed. "Mom, has something happened?"

"Yes. It's Dad. He had a heart attack this morning. I rushed him to the emergency room and the doctors stabilized him. Cam, do you think you could come home for a few days?"

I don't hesitate before answering, "Absolutely, I'll be there as soon as I can, probably before noon." I'm also worried about Mom. She sounds frazzled which is not like her so, I add, "and, Mom, I can stay as long as you need or want me to."

Relief is evident in Mom's voice as she says, "Oh, Cam, that's wonderful. Dad is still restricted to using crutches because of the sprain and now with the heart attack, I just didn't know how I was going to manage."

I'm emotionally overcome by Mom's anxiety, "You don't have to do this alone. I'll be on my way as soon as I can get squared away here."

"I'll probably be at the hospital when you arrive."

"What hospital?"

"Our Lady of Mercy, Room 312."

"I'll come straight to the hospital and find you, Mom."

"I know you will. Drive safely, Son."

"I will, don't you worry about me."

Mom sighs, "Okay, but you be careful just the same. See you soon."

———————— ≋ ————————

AS SOON AS I end the call with Mom, I go to Prescott's office. He's hunkered over his desk writing feverishly. Even though the door is now open, I knock; Prescott looks up, "Come in, Cam. I'm just finishing this chapter..."

I cut him off mid-sentence. It felt good to be on the other end for once. *Wonder how he likes being disrespected?* "Mr. Prescott, I just talked to my mother. My father had a heart attack this morning and I need to go home for a week, maybe longer..."

"Oh. That's too bad," Prescott says and, not bothering to disguise his irritation, he picks up a stack of handwritten manuscript and ruffles his thumb through the pages. "I was in hopes you could get this transcribed today."

"I'm sorry, but my parents need me right now."

"Of course, I understand." Prescott says, looking dejected.

Hope he doesn't interpret my crisis as another rejection. I know the consequences.

Prescott thoughtfully rubs his chin with his thumb and forefinger, "Wonder if Nikki would agree to fill in for you while you're gone?"

Oh, no! Now what do I do. "Ah, I don't think so. She's pretty busy working on her thesis..."

"That so? Think I'll give her a call, anyway," Prescott says, as he picks up the phone.

I stand helplessly by listening to Prescott's end of the conversation. It sounds like Nikki isn't too enthused about coming back to work for Prescott but, in the end, he wins her over.

Prescott ends the call and looks up at me, "Okay, that's settled. Nikki will be here later this afternoon. You go on home and stay as long as you need to." He then turns his attention back to his manuscript.

That's pretty cold, you narcissistic son-of-a-bitch. I go to my quarters and immediately call Nikki,

"Cam, what happened?" she says as soon as she picks up my call.

I explain to her the circumstances. "Nikki, I'm so sorry...I tried to dissuade him..."

"Nonsense, don't you even think about going there, you have nothing to apologize for and none of this is your doing. You need to put your parents' welfare first—I would. I think I can tolerate Prescott for a week or so."

"But...suspecting what we suspect..."

"He doesn't know that." After a pause, Nikki adds, "In high school, I was a *Thespian.* I evolved into a pretty good actress, I'll be all right. You go and stay as long as you need to," then after another pause, Nikki adds, "I'll be here when you get back."

That little comment lifts me, both spiritually and mentally. When we end our call, I hurriedly pack a few things. I won't need much as most of my clothes are still at home. When I'm ready to leave, I go past Prescott's office and look in. He's still bent over his desk writing as fast as he can.

"I'm leaving now, Mr. Prescott. I'll probably be gone a week or so."

"Okay. Have a safe trip," he says without even looking up. I resist the urge to slam the front door on my way out.

AS SOON AS I get on the interstate and head for the Keys, I'm feeling better; this is familiar territory. The highway parallels the Atlantic most of the way; the sky is clear and blue and the waves, topped with frothy whitecaps, rush to shore. Under different circumstances, I could enjoy the break from the Prescott nightmare. The trip usually takes four hours but, since I'm anxious to get home, I put the pedal to the metal whenever I feel it's safe to do so and make it home in a little over three.

WHEN I ARRIVE in Key West, I go immediately to Our Lady of Mercy hospital where a candy-striper directs me to Dad's room. I find Mom sitting by his bedside holding his hand. I'm appalled by her appearance; worry and lack of sleep have taken their toll. I walk over, caress her shoulders with my hands and kiss the top of her head.

"Hey, Mom," I say, "how's he doing?"

"Cam! You made it." Mom reaches up and, grabbing my left hand, she presses it affectionately against her cheek. She looks at me and then back down at Dad. "He's past the worst of it and the doctor says, *if* he behaves, he still has a long life ahead of him."

I nod. "Convincing Dad of lifestyle changes can be a challenge," I say.

"I know, but I think this scared him enough that he will be willing to slow down. We don't need another twenty million in the bank."

I'm stunned. *Didn't know my folks were so well off. Maybe I should reexamine my choice of careers.*

MOM AND I take shifts staying at Dad's bedside and I'm amazed at how quickly Dad recovers. Dad's doctor, Ulysses Somerton, is even impressed. Dad's allowed to leave the hospital after a three-day stay when Mom guarantees Dr. Somerton she will strictly enforce his orders. I overheard Somerton tell Mom that Dad could be the *poster child* for the benefits of keeping active and physically fit. Even after his ordeal, Dad looks better than either Mom or me.

Although Dad appears to be rebounding nicely, I opt to stay at home for the rest of the week just to make sure my parents are going to be all right. I don't feel like I have a choice. However, I'm conflicted realizing Nikki hates being there with Prescott. I send her an email.

Hey, Nikki!

> *I sincerely hope everything is going as well there as it is here. Dad's doctor released Dad from the hospital today. Doctor is amazed that 'the old codger' is doing so well. However, Mom is still anxious so I've decided to stay to the end of the week to ensure that they are both going to be all right.*

> *Looking forward to seeing you real soon.*
> *Cam*

The next morning I have a reply from Nikki.

Cam,

That's great news about your Dad. Of course your Mom is worried sick, I know I would be if I were her. You stay as long as you need to. I've got you covered here.

Looking forward to your return...for lots of reasons,

Nikki

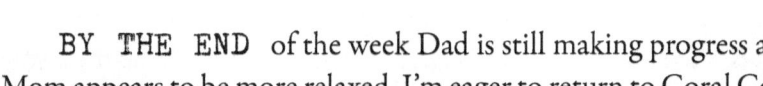

BY THE END of the week Dad is still making progress and Mom appears to be more relaxed. I'm eager to return to Coral Cove so I say, "Mom, it looks like you've got things under control here. I'm thinking of leaving tomorrow."

"Of course, Cam. I know Mr. Prescott needs you back." Mom steps up and embraces me in a warm hug, "Your being here has made all the difference in the world..."

"Wild horses couldn't have kept me away," I hug her back, "but don't underestimate your strength. You handled all of us like a real trooper. I just followed your lead."

THE NEXT MORNING I'm headed back to Coral Cove before the sun comes up. When I reach the city, I first stop at Nikki's. Having phoned ahead, I find Nikki waiting for me on the veranda. As I pull into the driveway she runs down the steps to greet me and I jump from the car and welcome her with open arms; we share a warm hug.

"Oh, Cam! I'm so happy you're back."

"Me, too." We're standing with our hands clasped in Nikki's driveway. I'm so overwhelmed to be back together that I pull her closer and kiss her warm, moist lips; she returns my kiss.

Seconds pass and the moment turns awkward. Nikki steps back away from me and asks, "How's your father doing?"

"Amazing."

"And Mom?"

"She's hanging in there." I look at Nikki as if seeing her for the first time. I'd almost forgotten how beautiful she is. "How are things here?" I finally manage to say.

"If you're referring to our mutual friend, the work is going well but..."

My heart stops, "But what!"

"This is a show and tell situation. When does Prescott expect you to return?"

"I didn't give him an exact time, only sometime today." I gently grab her by the arm; my fears are mounting, "What happened? Did he hurt or threaten you?"

"Oh no! Nothing like that." Nikki takes my hand, "Come on into the house. I want to show you something."

Now I'm the one experiencing anxiety over being kept waiting for details. When we enter the house, Nikki picks up a folder from a table in the foyer and leads me out onto a deck facing the ocean. Once we're seated, she opens the folder. I recognize the yellow paper as the kind Prescott uses. "Here, read this," Nikki says and takes a few sheets from the folder and hands them to me.

I look at the page number and date Prescott has written at the top. He prepared these pages the same day I left for the Keys. I raise my eyes to meet Nikki's. She nods toward the manuscript indicating for me to continue reading.

As I glance down at the first page, I recognize immediately that this is a depiction of a crime; it's violent and graphic—it's almost too much. I'm sickened by the brutality displayed in Prescott's writing. While I read through his scribbling, something about the murder nags at me. *Seems familiar—like I've heard this somewhere before.* Then it hits me, the Coral Cove murder. *That bastard! He's taken an actual homicide and engineered it to coincide with his novel. Did he kill that woman? What kind of monster would do that and then recreate the crime in his novel!*

I drop the pages onto my lap and look up. Nikki is focusing on my reaction.

Trying not to believe what I'm thinking, I run my hands through my hair. "Although we suspected something, I didn't want to believe he actually did it," I manage to sputter.

"Nor did I," Nikki says. "After all, since his rendition tracks the account from the *Gazette,* I'm more inclined to believe his only crime is being a copycat."

I'm speechless. I don't agree with Nikki's belief that Prescott didn't kill Kingston but I don't say so. I have to admit that Prescott's description of the murder deviated somewhat from the newspaper's account but not by much; probably just enough for a reader, after the novel is published some months from now, not to make a connection. He also added some *color* of his own by having the victim knock over a canister of flour during the death struggle. Prescott's description of the horror on the face of the dying woman is so realistic, it sends chills up my spine.

I LOOK UP and see Nikki staring at me, she asks, "What do you think we should do?"

"I don't know," I respond.

We sit in silence for a few moments. Nikki finally says, "Cam, let me play *Devil's Advocate* so we can analyze the situation."

I protest, "It's not just a coinci..."

"Just hear me out," Nikki interrupts. "Suppose Prescott has run out of plots and is desperate to get another novel published. When he reads the account of the murder in the newspaper, he seizes the opportunity to incorporate it into a plot."

I rub my face with my hands and respond, "I suppose that could be the case, but I'm not convinced. You didn't see that look in his eyes when he read the article to me the day after the homicide..."

"I agree. You have firsthand experience dealing with him regarding this but...but... accusing him of murder is a big jump from just suspecting he's involved—especially without any real evidence."

"I wasn't going to go to the authorities—at least not yet. I'm just trying to figure it all out. I don't want to believe he killed that woman but..."

"Neither do I," Nikki whispers.

Then something occurs to me. I ask, "When you told me he said 'I'll show 'er,' do you know who he was talking about?"

"No. Not a clue. Most likely someone at the *Shahrazad* book signing."

"Do you remember what date that was?"

"Yes. It was the last day I worked for him. Friday, January 15."

"About ten weeks ago..."

"That's right."

"Did he say what set him off?"

"H-m-m-m, about all I could understand from his rantings was '...believable, I'll show 'er believable.'"

Just then, Nikki's eyes grow wide and it appears to finally have hit her; he orchestrated the murder to create a *believable* crime.

Nikki grabs my hand, "Cam..."

"I know," I mumble, "I know."

Nikki and I are unable to come up with a viable solution to our dilemma. We have absolutely no concrete evidence to warrant alienating Prescott by telling law enforcement of our suspicions. We also have reason to believe he might eliminate us to cover his tracks.

"I don't see how we can pursue this," I say to Nikki. "And even though Prescott is a celebrity and thus a public figure, he can still sue us for defamation of character."

Nikki remains somber. Finally she asks, "Could we telephone the police anonymously? You know, just say our piece and hang up."

I ponder her suggestion for a few moments, and then say, "Don't think it would do any good. He's too smart to leave anything to chance. Judging by the amount of research on his desk, he's probably covered all the bases."

"So what *do* we do?"

"Well," I hesitate. "I'm not a coward but don't you think he would be able to ascertain where the anonymous tip came from? After all, how many people are privy to his inner sanctum?"

Nikki nods her head. "You're right. I didn't think it through. Then he'd probably come after us."

"Exactly. After you commit the first murder, if it was his first, what's another couple of notches on his belt?"

"Oh, my God! What *do* we do, Cam?"

"For the present, nothing." Then I confess, "Nikki, before I left home this morning I was tempted not to come back. I decided I could take the semester over in the fall to get my degree. Prescott treats me like a servant and I've grown to resent him. As if his calloused attitude toward the disappearance of Goliath wasn't enough, now we suspect he has the propensity to take the life of another human to create believable scenes in his novels."

Nikki reaches over and gently rubs my back, encouraging me to continue.

"Then, I thought I was probably overreacting because of my dislike for him." I stop and look up gazing out over the ocean, collecting my thoughts.

"So, what made you change your mind?"

I turn and look into her eyes, "You're the only reason I returned."

"Oh, Cam..."

"So, my dear, I put my decision on hold until I could meet with you."

"Why me?"

"Well, since you were closely associated with Prescott, I thought by brainstorming with you, you could convince me that I'm full of it. Now, after what we've discovered, I'm sure he murdered Kingston." I pause momentarily, then add, "And, besides, I like you."

Nikki blushes, "I like you, too." Nikki then looks up and says, "Dad's gone fishing with some of his cronies from town. He won't be back anytime soon."

I recognize an invitation when I hear one so I take Nikki's hand and lead her toward the house. "Don't believe I've ever seen your ancestral cottage. Care to give me a tour?"

"Why, I'd love to," Nikki chirps and then takes the lead. Slowly walking from room to room and in true tour guide fashion, Nikki describes the interior of the house. "This is the kitchen; this is the dining room; this is the pantry; and this is my room."

I step into Nikki's room and pull her in after me. Taking her into my arms, I whisper, "I missed you more that words can say."

"And I you," she whispers back.

BURIED AT SEA

I notice Prescott observing me very closely since my return from the Keys. Not sure if he realizes I've become suspicious of him. I try to act normal but my nerves are shattered and I jump at every loud noise.

Thankfully, there are only two weeks left in the internship. Prescott's novel is almost finished. He finally christened it *Beguiled,* and I have to admit that I like the title; it fits the plot perfectly. Although I still suspect that Prescott is a killer, I haven't been able to unearth any more clues pointing in that direction. Actually, all I have to go on is a gut-feeling and I'd look like a fool if I go to the authorities on a hunch. He could always admit that he did use real homicide circumstances to create a fictional murder and in all likelihood, would say, "last I heard, that isn't a crime."

I'm impatient for the semester to end and have already started packing. As I cram my belongings into the duffels, once again I'm conflicted. Several times since my return from the Keys, I've noticed that darkness cross Prescott's face as he follows me with his eyes. My fear is that, when I return to the Keys, Nikki will be vulnerable. I'm sure if Prescott thinks I suspect him of killing the Kingston woman, he must also suspect that Nikki and I have a shared opinion.

LOST IN MY thoughts, I sit at my desk staring out at the Atlantic as the setting sun slips below the horizon and twilight takes the helm. My nerves are so jagged that when Prescott enters, slamming my door open, my heart starts thumping so loudly, I barely hear him as he says, "Well, Cam, here it is. The epilogue! We're there, we made it," and he plops several handwritten sheets into my in-basket.

I manage a weak, "Fantastic."

"When you finish transcribing the final pages, we'll crack a bottle of champagne and celebrate. I think I'll call Nikki and have her come join us."

"But..." he's out the door and gone before I can protest. Constantly cutting me off before I can finish my sentences is particularly frustrating. Guess he can't waste his time listening to me because whatever I have to say just couldn't be very important. After all, I'm just an intern and a minion.

As soon as the door closes, I grab my cellphone. I want to warn Nikki. However, in my haste, I fumble the numbers and have to start over. My hopes of dissuading her from accepting his invitation before he has a chance to talk to her quickly vanish when my call goes to voicemail. *Dammit! The bastard beat me to it.*

At this juncture, I'm compelled to keep up the charade. I transcribe the epilogue and print the pages. When I check the counter on the bottom left hand side of my computer, it tells me he has 420 pages and 94,429 words. That's a pretty good sized book. I write this information on a Post-It Note, append it to the first page of the epilogue and take the finished product to his office. When I appear in his open doorway, he waves me in. I hand the typewritten pages to him and watch as he raises his eyebrows upon seeing the final tally. He turns and retrieves the rest of the manuscript from a locked drawer in his desk and adds the epilogue to it.

As he rifles through the completed project, he looks up at me, "I've enjoyed having you as an intern, Cam," he says and smiles but his smile doesn't touch his eyes. "My hope is that your time here has been beneficial to you as well and that you learned what the program is engineered to provide."

"Yes, yes, I have learned quite a lot." I pause searching my paralyzed brain for something positive to add. "Ah, it's been an experience of a lifetime."

"Why thank you, I consider your comments a compliment," Prescott responds and squints at me.

In his arrogance, he's probably musing that an untrained, unimportant, insignificant nobody has the audacity to evaluate his work. I keep pouring it on, "That's the reason I jumped at the chance to intern with you. However, in my humble opinion, I believe *Beguiled* is by far your best." I watch him smile broadly in response to my flattery. I continue, "You better get the sign painter lined up to change *IV* to *V* on *Best Seller's* bow. I'm honored to have been part of *Beguiled's* creation."

"Well, I'm humbled that you think so. Thank you very much." Prescott says as he places the manuscript back into his desk and locks the drawer, "You know the old adage, 'practice makes perfect' and that applies to authors as well." He looks up, "Nikki should be here soon. I thought we'd have our little celebration aboard *Best Seller IV*," he laughs, then adds, "That is before I change her name to *Best Seller V,* provided your prediction is correct."

My brain is whirling searching for a way to get us out of Prescott's little tête-à-tête. In order to keep him distracted, I ask, "Have you ever wondered why ships are referred to as *she* or *her?*"

"Ho-ho! That's a darn good question and the answer is yes." Adjusting his glasses, he continues, "After purchasing my cruiser, I researched the origin of the gender designation because I, too, was curious. When I read the explanation, I had to laugh." Prescott then opens a desk drawer, and after a short search, hands me a page that looks like he printed it from the Internet. It reads:

> A ship is called she because there is always a great deal of bustle around her; there is usually a gang of men about; she has a waist and stays; it takes a lot of paint to keep her looking good and it's not the initial expense that breaks you, it's the upkeep...
>
> Glossophilia

Prescott smiles, as he takes the page back, "That pretty much defines *my Best Seller.*" Before I can reply, I hear Nikki come in. When she enters Prescott's office, she says, "What's up? The two of you look pretty mysterious."

Prescott laughs, "I wanted to surprise you. We've just put the finishing touches on *Beguiled* and we're getting ready for a champagne toast. I wanted to include you since you were kind enough to take up the slack when Cam had to return home."

Nikki looks at me. When she stiffens, I know that she has registered the concern I have regarding this *celebration.*

Before either of us can say anything, Prescott stands and moves toward the door motioning for us to follow, "I went out earlier and put the bubbly on ice. Come on, let's get to it!"

WE WALK THE short distance from the residence to the pier. *Best Seller IV* rocks gently on the tide and as we approach, I see that Prescott has a couple of hurricane candles and an ice bucket set on a bench that doubles as a table. That uneasy feeling I experienced earlier has suddenly evolved into dread. I look up at the dark clouds that are gathering in the east and try not to expose my panic.

"Looks like a storm brewing," I say, "maybe we should..."

Prescott cuts me off, "No worries. Relax! We'll be finished with our *celebration* long before the weather turns hostile."

The way he said *celebration* caused the hair on the back of my neck to tingle. Nikki grabs my hand and I sense that she, too, is on the verge of panic.

When we reach *Best Seller IV,* I jump onto the stern and then hold out a hand to help Nikki aboard. *Yeah, like Nikki needs my help. She could twist me into a pretzel three times over before I knew what hit me.* Prescott has already positioned himself on one of the benches adjacent to the table. He has three champagne glasses lined up and when he opens the bottle, I involuntarily jump at the pop the cork makes as it zooms into oblivion.

Prescott grins and motioning to us, says, "Grab a seat, you two," and pours champagne into the glasses. Nikki and I sit down opposite him. I watch as he carefully selects which glasses to hand to us. Red flags are shooting up all over the place.

Prescott hands us each a glass and stands, "Here's to the finished product," then he looks at us, "and to you who helped make it possible." He raises his glass in salute and drains it. Nikki and I take a sip of bubbly. No loaded gun here and I'm feeling guilty and foolish for my suspicions and all the cloak and dagger nonsense. I'm moved to make a toast of my own and as I begin to stand, I waver. *What the heck...* Then it hits me. *That bastard slipped us a mickey...* Before I can form another thought, Nikki goes limp and slumps over onto my lap and then I, too, lose consciousness.

WHEN I REVIVE, I see Prescott on the bridge speeding full throttle out into open waters. He occasionally looks back at us and laughs maniacally as the wind whips his hair. Quite obviously, the man has lost his mind. We're lying on the deck, gagged and bound hand and foot. I look over at Nikki; she's struggling trying to free herself from the ropes. There's no doubt about Prescott's intentions.

When the cruiser begins to slow, I estimate we're probably ten miles from shore and minutes from death.

Suddenly, Prescott cuts the engine. *Here it comes.* I begin to thrash about, also struggling with the ropes. *If this is it, I'm not going down without a fight.* I watch Nikki's eyes grow wide with fear and, because of my fear of water, I, too, am terrified.

Prescott approaches us with his gun in one hand and a fish-cleaning knife in the other. He reaches down with the knife and cuts the ropes on Nikki's wrists and ankles. "Don't move!" he orders and then approaches me. Nikki, disregarding his 'don't move' order, rips the gag from her mouth as soon as her hands are free. However, she wisely doesn't say anything. Prescott shrugs, "Scream all you want. There's no one to hear you this far out." He then cuts the ropes binding me and says as he backs away from us, "Stand up, both of you and move to the railing, nice and easy." Prescott gestures toward the starboard side with his gun. "Don't try anything funny; we don't want any bruising or bullet holes to cause the medical examiner concern, now, do we?" I struggle up and stagger to a stand, the after-effect of the drug is making me woozy and having been bound for so long, my legs don't want to support me. I look at Nikki; she, too, is wavering.

When we finally make it to the starboard railing, everything happens so fast, I don't have time to think, I just react. Prescott viciously shoves Nikki over the side of the cruiser into the ocean. Then as he lunges at me, I grab him, catching the hand that's holding the gun. He loses his balance, firing a wild shot into the night and we both plummet over the railing into the cold, dark Atlantic. Somewhere in the annals of my memory I hear Dad telling me not to panic. However, remaining calm is not an option in this situation and when I hit the water, I begin wildly splashing around trying to stay afloat.

Off to my right, I hear Prescott screaming, "HELP, I can't swim! Please, help me!" I turn my head in his direction just in time to see an upstretched arm sink below the ocean's surface. I was in the throes of having my own panic attack so I couldn't have helped him, even if I wanted to. My struggling, laced with panic, soon exhausts me and I am about to give up and join Prescott in Davy Jones' locker, when suddenly I feel someone grab the back collar of my shirt. *Nikki?* In my stupor, I grab for her but I can't reach that far back without sinking.

My savior, still holding the back of my shirt collar, dunks me, apparently to get my attention. It works. When I resurface, even though water is streaming from my face and into my ears, I recognize Nikki's voice.

"Quit struggling, dammit, quit struggling!" Not wanting to go under again, I comply and literally force myself to go limp.

I soon feel Nikki pulling me backwards toward the stern of the boat. I'm on my back and have the presence of mind to begin kicking my legs helping move myself along. When we reach the stern, Nikki shouts, "GRAB HOLD," and shoves me toward the ladder that extends from the stern into the water. I lurch forward and frantically grab hold of a rung. Hooking my bent elbow through the rung, I pull my upper body up from the water and look back at Nikki. Instead of following me to safety, when she sees that I'm secure, she swims away toward where we last saw Prescott.

"NO! Nikki, he went under..." I say, getting a mouth full of water. It appeared as though she didn't hear me; she was moving swiftly away.

I drop my forehead against the arm that's still clinging to the ladder. There's not enough of me left to try to help rescue Prescott; I'm spent, physically and emotionally. Feeling like I weigh five hundred pounds, I lumber up the ladder and fall face first onto the deck. I'm so relieved to be on something solid, I don't even notice that, when I hit my face on the deck, the fall caused my nose to start bleeding. Streaming blood, I claw my way to the starboard railing screaming "NIKKI!" I pull myself up and lean out as far as I can hoping to see her. Nothing, there's no sign of her. I race to the port side and I call her name several times. No answer. *Please, God, don't let Nikki die.*

Standing at the railing, anxiously twisting my head back and forth looking for signs of Nikki, I frantically search the surrounding sea. Thunder claps overhead startle me and, when I jump back, I feel something wet and cold press against me. Panic seizes me. *I'm not going back into the ocean, at least not alive.* As I whip around prepared to defend myself, I careen into Nikki who is standing beside me peering into the black undulating water.

"NIKKI!" I cry, and wrap her in an embrace.

"Co...couldn't find Pres...cott," she stammers. Her teeth are chattering and she's shaking all over. "Maybe I...I should try again..."

"NO! You've already risked your life to save mine and made a valiant effort to save his." I pause briefly before adding, "If I'm worth dying for, then I'm worth living for."

Nikki nods and slumps down on one of the benches. She's shivering uncontrollably as she pulls her legs up, rests her head on her bent knees. I fear hypothermia is setting in and I race to the cabin, grab a blanket, race back and bundle her up, cradling her as close as I can sharing my body heat with her.

When I pull her into me, she buries her face against my chest and begins to sob. "Cam, he, he tried to kill us...he was going to kill us."

I hold her for a few minutes and whisper words of encouragement in an effort to comfort her. When her sobs subside, I go to the bridge, take the helm and turn the craft around. Nikki, still wrapped in the blanket, comes and stands beside me as I navigate toward shore. When she puts her hand on my shoulder, I reach up and cover it with mine. "Thank you, Nikki, for saving my life."

She squeezes my shoulder then sits down next to me.

ON THE WAY back to shore, Nikki and I brainstorm on how we're going to report the *accident*. We agree not to mention our suspicions that Prescott murdered Lisette Kingston. After all, we have no proof and with Prescott now dead, we'd look pretty foolish. Prescott was famous which made him a local celebrity, and the fact that a bestselling author lived in Coral Cove, put the quaint little town on the map. We're just college students and I'm an interloper, at that.

Our contrived story is that Prescott invited us to go on a short cruise to celebrate the end of my internship since I was to leave in the next couple of days. He also wanted to thank Nikki for her clerical help prior to my coming. He planned a champagne celebration aboard his cruiser for both of us.

When we were about ten miles from shore, Prescott cracked the champagne and poured us each a glass. He then stood on one of the benches in the stern and raised his glass to make a toast. As he did so, we were suddenly hit by a large wave that rocked the boat. Prescott was immediately flung over the side into the ocean. I was thrown from the bench I was sitting on crashing my face onto the deck causing me to have a nose bleed. When finally the boat stopped rocking, we ran to the railing. There was no sign of Prescott; the ocean had swallowed him. At that point, the water was so rough that it would have been suicide to jump in and try to find him. We kept vigilance for about thirty minutes then gave up and came back here.

"Do you think the cops will believe our story?" Nikki asks.

"Don't know, but don't think we have a choice."

UPON REACHING PRESCOTT'S pier, I maneuver *Best Seller IV* into her slot and once she is secured, Nikki and I go to the house and I call the Coral Cove police to report an accidental drowning. Shortly after I make the call, two uniformed officers arrive. I take the lead and introduce us, "I'm Camron Donovan and this is Nikki Palmer..."

Putting his thumb against his chest, one of the officers says, "Officer Joseph Tanner." He then points to his partner, "Officer Sam Cummings. Do you have ID?"

I look at Nikki and she shakes her head. "I don't have mine with me," she says to Tanner. "I live about three miles up the beach..."

"Okay," Tanner says, scribbling on a notepad he retrieved from his breast pocket, "we'll get yours later." Then he looks at me," And you?"

"Yes, I'll go get my driver's license, it's in my room."

As I turn to leave, Tanner says, "Hold it! Sam'll go with you," and nods at Officer Cummings.

Cummings puts the flashlight he had been holding in a loop on his police duty belt and gestures for me to lead the way. Before leaving the room, I glance at Nikki; she looks haggard and is nervously twisting a tissue. *Oh, my God. I hope she holds up and sticks to our story.* I quickly walk to my quarters with Cummings close behind and extract my driver's license from my wallet. When I hand it to Officer Cummings, he carefully inspects it and records my information on a small notepad he takes from *his* breast pocket. We rejoin Nikki and Officer Tanner in the foyer and I hear Tanner ask Nikki, "Okay, from the beginning, what's this all about?" I notice both officers have their pens and pads at the ready,

Apparently, Nikki hasn't said too much in my absence because when Cummings and I reenter the room, she gestures to me, "Well, you see, Cam and I..."

Tanner sharply looks in my direction. He says to Nikki, "Hold it right there." He then says to Cummings, "Take Donovan into another room and get his story."

Fear grips me. *Do they suspect something?*

Cummings takes my arm and ushers me into the kitchen. Once we're settled, I tell him our contrived version of what happened. He takes notes and occasionally nods but doesn't say anything. At the conclusion of my rendition, we're joined by Nikki and Tanner.

Tanner asks, "Are there any relatives that need to be notified?"

I look at Nikki. She shakes her head. I respond, "No, or at least none that we're aware of. I haven't known Mr. Prescott too long. However, I've seen a rolodex on his desk. You may find someone listed there."

Tanner turns to Cummings, "Take the rolodex to the station for examination." Then he turns back to me, "Where's the boat now?"

"Docked at the pier just down there," I point to where *Best Seller IV* is moored.

"Okay, show us," Tanner says.

I turn on the outside lights and we all go out the sliding glass doors, across the patio down to the dock. The officers use their flashlights to do a cursory examination of the boat as Nikki and I wait at the edge of the pier. I squeeze Nikki's hand and she squeezes back. I take that as confirmation that she told the contrived version of our involvement.

After a few minutes, the officers are back. "You say you were about ten miles out when the accident occurred?" Tanner asks.

"Yes," Nikki and I say in unison.

Tanner points to the blood on the deck and looks at us.

"That's from my nose bleed," I say, before he can ask, and point to my scraped nose.

"Right," he grunts and squints at the scrape.

He pauses momentarily and, putting his hands on his hips, looks around the surrounding area and says, "Okay. I think we can wrap this up. There's nothing we can do to retrieve the body. No telling where or when it will wash ashore from ten miles out." As he closes and stores the notepad in his breast pocket, he continues,

"We'll make the report. The captain will want the two of you to come to the station to make a formal statement."

I relax. I can breathe again, "Okay," I say. "When?"

"Tomorrow morning. You won't need an appointment, just show up. And, I suspect you know the drill...don't leave town without clearing it through us," Tanner says and looks directly at me.

"Okay," then I add, "when I'm not in school, I live with my parents in the Keys. You have the address, it's on my driver's license."

"Okay. So, what are you doing here?" Tanner asks.

"Like I told Officer Cummings, Prescott volunteered to mentor me and invited me to stay here during my internship." I pause briefly and then ask, "Since I've been living here, is it okay if I stay until you approve of my leaving?"

Tanner looks at Cummings and shrugs. Cummings nods. Tanner says, "Sure." Then he looks at Nikki, "Come on, we'll take you home."

I intervene before Nikki can say anything. "Would it be all right if I take her home? I, ah, I want to be there when she explains to her father what happened." What I really want is a chance for us to compare notes before we go to the station tomorrow.

Nikki nods, conveying her consent for me to take her home. I assume she also wants to compare notes.

"Sure, I don't have a problem with that," Tanner says and turns toward the front door. Cummings follows. I go to the door with them and see them out.

WHEN I RETURN to the living room, Nikki is sitting on the sofa with her legs curled up beneath her. I'm an exhausted wreck and I slump down on the chair opposite. After a few awkward moments, I ask, "What do you think?"

Nikki looks thoughtful before answering. "I don't know why they won't believe us. I stuck to the story, chapter and verse."

"So did I and *Best Seller IV* squared with our story." I lean forward and bracing my elbows on my knees, clasp my hands under my chin supporting my weary head and say, "I'm glad they separated us. That'll give more credibility to our statements."

Nikki frowns and looks around. "This place feels strange, almost haunted. With Goliath's disappearance and now with Prescott dead, I get an uneasy feeling just being here."

"It's just a nervous reaction," I say. "You've been through quite an ordeal these last few hours..."

"As well as you," she says and then adds, "if you're not comfortable staying here, I'm sure Dad won't mind if you use the guest room for a few days."

I think about it for a moment. "I don't know. Since I told the police I'd be here, I think I should stay. Besides, I still have some packing to do."

"Okay, but if you don't mind, I'd like to go now. This place is giving me the creeps."

"Sure," I rise and hold out my hand to help her up.

When we arrive at Nikki's, she turns to me before exiting the Jetta, "Sure you won't change your mind about staying here?"

I laugh, "Right now, I'm sure. However, when the ghosts start prowling the corridors at midnight, I may change my mind."

Nikki punches my bicep and opens the passenger door. "What time do you want to go to the police station tomorrow?"

"Early, the sooner we get this behind us, the better. Say about nine?"

"I'll be ready," then she's gone. I watch her safely enter her home and then I leave.

MAYBE IT'S THE power of suggestion but, when I arrive back at Prescott's, I, too, feel the creepiness Nikki spoke of earlier this evening. I shake off the sensation and summon up the courage to proceed to my quarters. As I pass Prescott's office, I glance in and my eyes fall on his desk. I begin to remember the last conversation we had in this room concerning *Beguiled* and then watching him lock the manuscript in a desk drawer and hide the desk key in between the padded back and seat of his desk chair. *Guess now I know why he wasn't too concerned about revealing his hiding place to me. Dead men don't snoop and dead men don't talk.*

I walk around his desk, sit down in his chair, find the key and unlock the drawer. I stare at the manuscript for long moments, feeling as though I'm in a trance. I gently remove it from the drawer and caress it. *What if...what if I use my name to publish* Beguiled... *NO! That would be plagiarism and that's illegal....but... it's illegal only if I get caught.*

I roughly toss the manuscript back into the drawer and slam the drawer shut. However, closing the drawer doesn't quell the temptation. I can't stop thinking about the manuscript. I finally yield to the urge and, rubbing my brow, I mentally start planning my strategy. *I'll wait at least six months, maybe a year, to publish it. Then I'll change the title, the names of the characters and, of course, the name of the author. Prescott told me that once you're on the bestseller list, your subsequent novels sell like crazy.* Beguiled *could be that stepping stone for me. I'll work on a novel of my own while I'm waiting to publish* Beguiled...*and thanks to Prescott's antics, I have a perfect plot for my creation. Truth is indeed stranger than fiction.*

I retrieve the manuscript once again from the drawer and rifle through the pages. *Prescott was paranoid—always afraid someone would pilfer his plots so he kept them a closely guarded secret. He even swore me to secrecy. No one, other than Nikki, knows about* Beguiled. *And, Nikki was involved in only one chapter, the part of the novel she transcribed when I went home. If it becomes an issue, I can always claim that I liked the scene so much that I decided to use it in my own novel.*

As soon as I get to my room, I transfer a copy of the manuscript onto a flash drive and also email a copy to my home computer in the Keys. I then delete it from Prescott's computer and take the paper copy out to the patio where I start a fire in the fire pit and burn it down to white ash. While I wait for the fire to die down, I look out at the Atlantic. *I know you killed Kingston and probably Goliath, and tried to kill Nikki and me, you bastard! Rot in hell!* I then point to the fire pit and say aloud, hoping Prescott can hear me from wherever he happens to be, "Serendipity!"

THE NEXT DAY when Nikki and I arrive at the Coral Cove police station, we're ushered into separate interrogation rooms. I'm left waiting for about ten minutes. I don't know what is transpiring with Nikki. However, on my end, the wait increases my apprehension and especially after my plan to plagiarize *Beguiled.* Sitting alone in the cold lackluster room, I'm spiritually, mentally and emotionally wrestling with my decision regarding the novel.

I'm so lost in my conflict that I actually jump when my interrogator enters the room and slams the door behind him. As he approaches, he nonchalantly tosses a manila folder onto the cold steel table and takes the chair opposite me. His attitude catches me off guard and increases my anxiety. *He acts like he suspects something isn't right.*

He smiles and holding out his hand, says, "I'm Detective Blake Corrigan."

I nod and shake his hand.

Corrigan then slides his chair closer to the table and opens the folder. "Can I get you some coffee or water?" he asks.

I relax. His seems to be sincere. "No, thank you. I'm good," I answer.

Corrigan nods and poises a pen above what looks like an official document. As he questions me regarding my personal information, he records my answers on a form. When the form is completed, he puts the pen back in his pocket and looks up, saying, "Okay, Cameron, tell me what happened. We're electronically recording your statement," he pauses and points to a camera affixed to one of the corners in the ceiling, then continues, "It will be transcribed for the file."

"File! What file?" I blurt.

Corrigan raises his eyebrows, "Easy, son, we keep files on all deaths we investigate, accidental or otherwise."

"Oh, I see." I try to relax as I repeat the story I told Officer Cummings the night before, hoping it doesn't sound contrived or rehearsed.

At the conclusion of my rendition, we both sit in silence for a few moments. Finally, Corrigan asks, "Do you have anything further to add to your statement?"

I ponder his question, then say, "No, I can't think of anything." *If they're suspicious, I don't think I could pass a lie detector test even though our story is partially true.*

I'm jerked back to the present when Corrigan stands, skidding his chair across the tile floor. I cringe; the noise has the same effect as scratching fingernails across a blackboard. Much to my relief Corrigan says, "Okay then, you're free to go."

"Free...Ah, thank you..." Then I ask, "Does that mean I can return to the Keys?"

Corrigan flips the folder open and looks at the form he had just filled out. After studying it for a few moments he says, "Yep. Looks like we have your Key West address and all the information we need for the present." He then offers me his hand again, and says, "Have a safe trip home."

We shake and I start for the door. However, he stops me before I can open it, "Here's my card," he says, "if anything else occurs to you, please call me."

"Yes, of course." I pause briefly, then ask, "Were you able to locate any relatives?"

"Yes, we were. There was a woman with the same last name listed in his rolodex. Turns out she's his sister, lives in Sydney, Australia. Apparently, she was a joint-owner of Prescott Mansion along with her brother and is making plans to arrive in order to settle the estate."

I nod and leave the interrogation room. I spot Nikki as I enter the lobby. When she sees me, she turns and smiles. Not wanting to appear too eager to leave, I casually walk to where she's standing and we exit the police station together.

Once outside I ask, "How'd it go?"

Nikki furrows her brow, "Hard to say. The questions were benign and I didn't detect anything out of the ordinary." Then she pauses, "Yep, like we'd know what 'ordinary' is in situations like this."

I smile at her innuendo, "Know what you mean. I didn't feel pressured, and I have permission to go home."

"That's wonderful. Releasing you, in-and-of-itself, is a huge relief."

"Right, but they know where to find me," I say in jest. Somehow, my joke doesn't seem that funny; neither of us laugh.

As we approach the Jetta, I pause at the passenger door before opening it for Nikki, "Guess that means we're not 'persons of interest.'"

"Well, why should we be? After all, we didn't do anything—he's the one who tried to kill us, remember?" Nikki says, then adds, "I found out that Prescott has a sister and she's on her way to Coral Cove."

I nod. "Detective Corrigan, my interviewer, told me that as well."

"Did he tell you that sister-dearest didn't appear the least bit upset when she learned of Prescott's demise?"

"No, he didn't mention that..."

"Apparently the officer who interviewed me, Detective Molly Ferguson, was acquainted with Hannah, Prescott's sister. She said that she went to school with Hannah and that they were close friends. Ferguson didn't elaborate but I got the impression that Prescott was pretty mean to Hannah."

"Doesn't surprise me in the least."

"Me neither." Then Nikki adds, "Ferguson alluded to the fact that she thought Hannah left Coral Cove because of Prescott. Seems that the estate belonged to their parents and they each inherited an equal share. Molly said there was a clause in the will stating that if either of them took up residence in the mansion, the other was barred from selling it until the sibling moved out or died."

I open the car door and as Nikki slips onto the leather seat, I say, "Nikki, if it weren't for having met you, I wish I'd never come here."

"Why, Cam, what a lovely thing to say. I, too, am glad we met," Nikki says and reaches up and kisses my cheek. She then adds, "Anyway, how were you to know any of this was going to happen?"

THE NEXT MORNING'S edition of the *Coral Chronical* carried the story of Prescott's accident: *LOCAL AUTHOR, ASHLAND PRESCOTT, LOST AT SEA*

> Local celebrity and author of four bestselling novels, Ashland Prescott, has been reported lost at sea. Cameron Donovan and Nikki Palmer, college students who worked for Prescott, told authorities that, while on a brief cruise aboard Prescott's yacht, Prescott was cast overboard when a large wave rocked the craft. His body has not yet been recovered.

Prescott authored four novels that made the New York Times Bestseller List. It is reported that Prescott had recently sold the movie rights on his latest work of fiction, The Wager.

Survivors include a sister, Hannah Prescott, a former Coral Cove resident who currently lives in Australia.

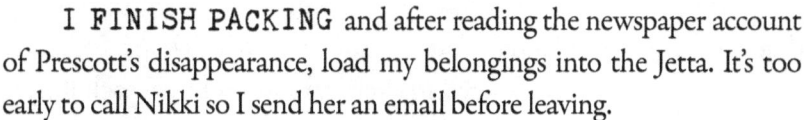

I FINISH PACKING and after reading the newspaper account of Prescott's disappearance, load my belongings into the Jetta. It's too early to call Nikki so I send her an email before leaving.

> *Nikki,*
>
> *I'm ready to leave much earlier than I expected. I think I'm sharing the creepiness you were experiencing the other night and the sooner I vacate this place, the better.*
>
> *I'll see you in two weeks when I return for graduation. Until then, take care.*
>
> *Cam*

I realize my email sounds cold, especially after all we've been through together. However, during my sleepless night, I wrestled with my feelings for Nikki. I finally decided that continuing a relationship with her would eventually expose me as a plagiarist so, at the end of the day, I decide to give her up.

FULL STEAM AHEAD

As soon as the graduation ceremonies are complete I say good-bye to Nikki. Mom, Dad and I return home to the Keys. After dinner, I barricade myself in my room. I'm anxious to make changes in Prescott's novel before anyone discovers it on my computer. I've given a lot of thought to what I would rename it and after careful consideration, I settle on *Jeopardy*. The new title has a *double entendre*. On the one hand, it's a perfect title for the novel and on the other, it describes the precarious position in which I place myself by taking credit for someone else's work.

This evening when I open the file, I begin to tremble. My hands shake when I touch the keyboard and change the title from *Beguiled* to *Jeopardy. Maybe I'm not cutout to be a criminal after all.* However, seeing the new title typewritten in big bold letters for the first time reinforces my resolve and then I immediately begin to rename the characters. With the revisions I've made so far, the novel is beginning to feel like mine and lastly, when I change the author's name from Ashland Prescott to Cameron Donovan, it suddenly *is* mine.

I sit back and stare at the computer monitor running a profusion of *what if's* through my addled brain. I conjure up situations which might call into question my authorship and prove detrimental. However, I work out a plausible explanation to each of my scenarios and convince myself that the pluses far outweigh the negatives. I also decide to wait at least a year before publishing *Jeopardy*. The wait will lessen the chance that anyone would tie *Jeopardy* to *Beguiled* and thus expose my deception. During the wait, I'll use the time to work on an independent novel of my own. With what I've learned from transcribing Prescott's writing and, of course, the real-life drama I recently lived through, I'm more than equipped to write the great American novel of which I've always dreamed. I smile when I think that a novel written by me may top *Mr.* Prescott's on the bestseller list—not to mention the fact that he not only inadvertently provided the plot but ended up being one of the main characters. *Serendipity!*

BEFORE I SHUT down my computer, I check my email. I have a message from Nikki. It reads:

> *Hey, Cam!*
>
> *Just checking to see that you made it home okay. I'm sorry you had to leave so suddenly.*
>
> *Congratulations on your commencement—job well done. After all you went through to get there, you deserve more than just a diploma and, you know what I mean.*
>
> *Warm wishes,*
> *Nikki*

My heart is heavy. However, since I've decided that Nikki is history, I don't respond.

THREE MONTHS HAVE passed and I'm assuming that since I haven't replied to any of Nikki's emails during that time is the reason she has stopped corresponding with me. *Brilliant deduction, Dr. Watson.* Hopefully, she's taken the hint and will forget about me. Though I miss her, I'm not tempted to relent.

I've been preoccupied with writing *my* novel and having an incredible plot virtually handed to me on a silver platter, I'm emotionally charged. The scenes play out in my head as though I'm reliving them. I'm almost at the halfway point when I notice Mom putting up Halloween decorations, I'm stunned at the passage of time. I've been so intrigued with writing that I barely notice the summer is turning into fall. I recall Dr. Charlesworth telling my journalism class that, "Writing is a jealous mistress—she demands all of your time and all of your attention." Now I know exactly what he had reference to.

My novel, which I chose to title *Sweet Revenge,* is taking on a personality all its own. Some days I can't type fast enough to keep up with my thoughts and, by the time Christmas rolls around, I'm completing the epilogue. When I type the last period, I experience mixed emotions. On one hand, I'm elated to have it finished, on the other, I'm sad that it's finished. I know in my heart that I'll never be able to create another story even close to this one. That is, of course, unless Prescott resurfaces.

I take a printed copy of *Sweet Revenge* out to the deck where I prop myself up in a lounge chair and begin the final editing. Mom soon joins me. She has in her hands a stack of Christmas cards she just retrieved from the mailbox. As she sorts through them, she tosses one onto my lap. I look at Mom and she raises her eyebrows. The card is from Nikki. I slowly open the envelope and extract the contents. It's a cute cartoon card with a variety of forest animals dancing around an evergreen shouting "Merry Christmas." The signature reads, "Hope your holidays are joyful, Nikki."

I set the card aside and direct my attention back to editing my manuscript, albeit under the scrutiny of mother's watchful eyes. I sense she's waiting for an explanation so I avoid her gaze by trying to look as though I'm in deep concentration. She finally gives up and goes into the house. After she leaves, I look again at the card. Sadness engulfs me and I feel like a heel for the way I dumped Nikki.

WHEN SPRING ARRIVES, I'm ready to start the publishing process for *Jeopardy*. I set *Sweet Revenge* aside for the time being. When *Jeopardy* reaches bestseller status, I'll publish *Sweet Revenge* knowing it, in all likelihood, will also top the charts. Once I'm established, anything I write will undoubtedly be a bestseller. At least, that appears to be the pattern.

I contact Keeley House, the publisher listed in Prescott's previous novels. The representative I talk to tells me they will review *Jeopardy* for possible publishing and get back to me. A few weeks after I submit the manuscript, I receive a packet from Keeley House. The transmittal letter reads:

Dear Mr. Donovan:

First, let me congratulate you on the excellent novel you submitted. It's very rare for a first time author to create a work of this caliber. We are pleased that you chose Keeley House to publish *Jeopardy*.

Regarding the publishing process, our protocol is that once the interior design and cover are established, we will create a hardcopy and corresponding eBook. We will then launch our patented marketing campaign including press releases to thousands of media outlets.

We will also produce a trailer which highlights the theme of your novel and create a webpage about you and your book and direct readers to links where they can purchase it. Our published works are distributed worldwide to over 50,000 outlets including retailers, libraries, schools and online sources.

Please review the contract and, if it meets with your approval, sign and return it in the enclosed envelope.

Regards,
Charlotte Hudson
Publishing Editor
Keeley House

jb

Enclosures

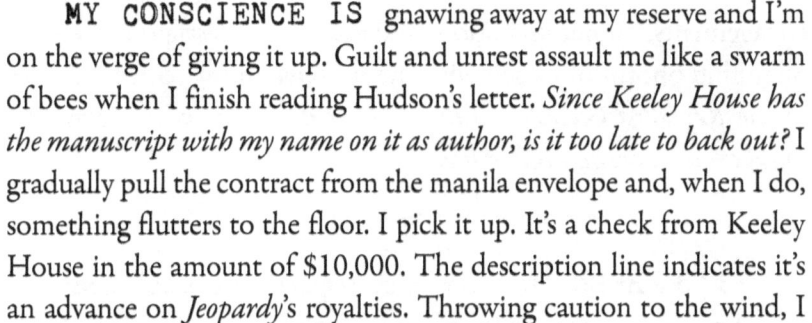

MY CONSCIENCE IS gnawing away at my reserve and I'm on the verge of giving it up. Guilt and unrest assault me like a swarm of bees when I finish reading Hudson's letter. *Since Keeley House has the manuscript with my name on it as author, is it too late to back out?* I gradually pull the contract from the manila envelope and, when I do, something flutters to the floor. I pick it up. It's a check from Keeley House in the amount of $10,000. The description line indicates it's an advance on *Jeopardy*'s royalties. Throwing caution to the wind, I immediately sign the contract and take it to the post office.

LAUNCHED

I'm not surprised when, as predicted, after a few months, *Jeopardy* reaches bestseller status. I've wrestled my demons down and put the plagiarism concern behind me. I'm now basking in the euphoria of being an author—a bestselling author, at that. I've been catapulted into the public eye and my life has drastically changed. My days and nights are now filled with book signings, speaking engagements, dinner invitations and attending prestigious events. I often find photos of myself with the *in crowd* in the society section of the *Key West Gazette. So this is what it's like to be a celebrity? I could get used to this kind of life.*

———————⟫———————

IT'S BEEN A year since *Jeopardy* was published and, now, I decide I've waited long enough and that it's time to publish *Sweet Revenge.*

I contact Charlotte Hudson at Keeley House regarding the publishing.

"Cameron," she says, bubbling over with enthusiasm, "how's the new novel coming?"

Although I've been sitting on it for a year, I say, "Just finished the final rewrite. That's what I'm phoning about. I think I'm ready to publish."

"WONDERFUL!"

I have to pull the phone away from my ear, her response is so loud.

"Ohhh, sorry," Charlotte says in a quieter tone. "I get carried away when I become excited." After a brief pause, she asks, "How soon can you get the manuscript to us?"

"All I have to do is push the send key and it's on its way."

"Then push away! I'll be waiting for it and I will personally handle the processing. What's the title?"

"*Sweet Revenge*," I answer.

"Catchy title. Is it a sequel to *Jeopardy*?"

"Ah, no, not really. Whole different plot and cast of characters."

"Hold on, I think I'm receiving it now." There's a slight pause and then Charlotte says, "Yes, yes, here it comes."

I breathe a sigh of relief. At least this novel is mine. "I am, of course, eager to get your opinion, Charlotte."

"I'm just perusing through the Prologue, Cameron, and, it looks like maybe it's another bestseller."

I smile. *Thought it might be.* "Time-wise, what do…"

"Let's see, today is Thursday. I'll have the contract ready by Monday assuming the rest of the novel is as good as the Prologue. Same terms, same advance. Meet with your approval?"

"Yep!"

"I'll overnight the paperwork on Monday. Once we receive the signed contract…hard copy in, let's say… eight to ten weeks."

When we end our conversation, I rear back and stare at the monitor. *Another bestseller! Eat your heart out, Prescott…that is, provided you ever had one.*

NIKKI WAS LOUNGING on the patio flipping through the *Key West Gazette* when she suddenly jerks upright. Her face flushes when she sees a picture of Cam in the society section looking very dapper holding a glass of champagne in one hand with a beautiful debutant hanging on his other arm. The caption reads: *Bestselling mystery author, Cameron Donovan...* Nikki angrily wads the newspaper in a ball and slings it across the patio. It had been over two years since she last saw or heard from Cam. *Guess this explains why he didn't have time for a nobody like me; looks like he's living it up in the Keys. Maybe I should buy a copy of his bestseller just to see how 'the great American novel' turned out. On the other hand, why give him the satisfaction.*

———————— ≈ ————————

MARJO CORRIGAN, DETECTIVE Blake Corrigan's wife, was an avid reader and being married to a homicide detective, relished mysteries. Marjo went immediately to the bookstore and picked up a copy of *Jeopardy* when she read in the *Key West Gazette's* book review section that it was written by a local author, Cameron Donovan. The book review went on to say that *Jeopardy* was a "thriller guaranteed to keep you in suspense until the very end." She especially enjoyed reading books by local authors and had read all four of Prescott's novels. She found it exciting when the author mentioned something in the novel that she recognized as being indigenous to her environment.

When Marjo returned home from the bookstore, as was her custom, she sequestered herself in a lounge chair by the pool where she spent quiet hours devouring the pages of her mysteries. The sun was waning in the west by the time Marjo was midway through *Jeopardy.* She glanced at her watch and knew she should start dinner but, intrigued by the upcoming murder scene, she was unable to set the novel aside so she continued reading. As the murder unfolded,

Marjo experienced something similar to that *déjà vu* feeling. The facts surrounding the murder seemed very familiar to her.

OVER DINNER THAT evening, Marjo mentions to her husband that the new novel she is reading more-or-less mirrors one of his unsolved murder cases.

"That right?" Corrigan manages to say through a mouthful of tuna casserole. His demeanor expresses little or no interest.

"Yes, that's right!" Marjo replies. Her husband's habit of dismissing or even outright ignoring anything she says was very irritating and the tone of her voice now conveys her irritation.

Corrigan, still cramming casserole in his mouth, says, "Want to tell me about it?"

"You sure you want me to? You usually ignore me."

"Ah, come on! I've had a rough day and don't need this from you, too."

"Okay, just forget it!" Clearly on agitation overload, Marjo stands and begins clearing the table jerking Corrigan's plate out from under him before he finishes his dinner.

Corrigan, finally catching the clue, leans over and gently takes her arm as she reaches for the salad bowl. He eases her back into her chair. "Sorry, honey. Didn't mean to come across as an ogre. Of course I want to hear about it. I'll help you with the cleanup." Then, attempting to lighten the situation and further interact with her, he adds, "What's for dessert?"

"Key lime pie, Quasimodo," Marjo says managing a smile. "I'll get the dishes, you go relax. This won't take long." Then she pauses, "In the meantime, perhaps you'd like to read the chapter I'm referring to."

"Sure," Corrigan replies, as he heads for his favorite recliner. *Anything to please her.*

Marjo retrieves her copy of *Jeopardy* and follows him into the living room. "Here ya go. I've bookmarked the chapter," she says and hands the novel to Corrigan.

Corrigan studies the cover for a moment and then turns the book over. When he sees the picture of Cameron Donovan on the back he looks up at Marjo. "Hey, I know this guy," he says.

"You do?"

"Yep! I interviewed him regarding the Prescott drowning.

Marjo sits down in the chair opposite her husband. "That's a coincidence."

"Humph! I don't believe in coincidences," Corrigan retorts as he opens *Jeopardy* to the place Marjo had bookmarked.

Marjo sits and watches Corrigan's face contort as he reads the designated pages. Ten minutes into his reading, he says, "I'll be dammed! This sounds a lot like the Kingston murder."

"Yes, that's right, Lisette Kingston. I couldn't remember her name," Marjo replies.

"Marjo, this guy knows as much, or even more, about the murder scene than I do." Then after a pause, Corrigan adds, "Go get your scrapbook."

Marjo kept a scrapbook throughout Corrigan's detective career. She clipped articles involving his cases and meticulously organized them chronologically in a three ring binder in plastic page savers. She now hurries to the bedroom and retrieves the scrapbook. When she hands it to him, he quickly pages through to articles from two years before. When he finds the ones he's seeking, he reads them aloud.

When he finishes he looks at Marjo, "You're a pretty fair detective, notice anything amiss?"

Marjo frowns, apparently thinking, "No... Wait! Yes! None of the articles mention the spilled canister of flour!"

"BINGO!" Corrigan reaches over and squeezes Marjo's hand. "Good work, my dear."

Marjo beams. "Thank you, darling..." But before she can finish her sentence, Corrigan is once again off in his own world.

THE NEXT DAY when Corrigan arrives at the Coral Cove police station, he calls a meeting of the detective squad. He had, of course, taken the copy of *Jeopardy* with him to work.

"Most of you undoubtedly recall the murder of Lisette Kingston almost two years ago." Nearly all of the detectives nod their heads. Holding Marjo's copy of *Jeopardy* up for them to see, he continues, "My wife, while reading this novel, discovered the murder scene depicted in the book mirrored the Kingston murder...exactly."

Sgt. Patrick Mahoney replies, "Okay, so what?"

"Well, Patrick, me lad, it appears that Donovan, the author," Corrigan points to the picture of the author on the back cover, "knew details that were never released to the public."

"Like what?" Mahoney asks.

"Like the canister of spilled flour..."

"Holy Mother of God! Let me see," Mahoney demands.

Corrigan proceeds to read the entire chapter to those assembled. At the end of his dissertation, Mahoney grunts, "We deliberately withheld that bit of information from the press." Then he rubs his chin, "It's almost like this Donovan guy was there in person."

"My thoughts exactly!" Corrigan pauses, then adds, "And, the plot thickens. Around the same time period one Ashland Prescott, bestselling author of several mystery novels, fell off his yacht and drowned. Officers Joe Tanner and Sam Cummings investigated the Prescott drowning. The next day, I interviewed Donovan who was aboard the yacht at the time of the drowning. Molly Ferguson interviewed a young woman who was also aboard at the time. Later the drowning was determined to be accidental. However, our man here, Donovan," Corrigan holds up the book again, stabbing the picture of Cam with a rigid forefinger, "was living with Prescott doing an internship when Prescott drowned."

"You don't say," Mahoney mutters.

"I do say and, I think we have enough to at least pick him up for questioning."

"You know where he is?" Detective Spence Gillespie asks.

"The bio on the back cover says he lives in Key West. We should still have a file on him which will, in all likelihood, contain his permanent address or that of a relative."

10

KEEL HAULED

Detectives Corrigan, Mahoney and Gillespie arrive at the Key West Police Department a little before noon. Sgt. Ramon Sanchez, previously advised of their arrival, greets them when they enter the lobby.

After introductions and handshakes all around, Sanchez asks, "Do you have the warrant?"

Corrigan taps his breast pocket with the fingers of his right hand, "Right here."

"Okay, I'm sending a couple of uniforms with you since the arrest will take place in our jurisdiction and since you're not familiar with the area."

"Thanks for all your help," Corrigan says and looks around, "How soon can we get started?"

"Right now." Sanchez motions for two uniformed officers to come forward.

The Coral Cove detectives follow the Key West officers to a ritzy oceanfront neighborhood. They approach Donovan's home and knock loudly on the door.

I **ANSWER THE** door and when I see the bevy of what appears to be police officers gathered outside my apartment, I suddenly feel weak. *Someone finally figured out I plagiarized Prescott's novel and now I'm in for it.*

"Yes." I finally manage to say.

"Are you Cameron Donovan?" Corrigan asks.

"Yes, what's this all about?" I stammer.

"I'm Detective Blake Corrigan of the Coral Cove Police Department. You and I met several years ago after the boating accident involving Ashland Prescott."

I look more closely at him. "Yes, I remember. You were one of the investigating officers. In fact, you were the one who interviewed me."

"That's right. I now have a warrant for your arrest."

"My arrest! For what? Prescott's drowning?"

"No, the murder of Lisette Kingston," Corrigan blurts.

I stagger backward almost falling down. "Lisette Kingston? I didn't even know her." I wobble to the sofa and plop down, rubbing my face with my hands. *The murder scene in Prescott's novel mirrored that of Lisette Kingston and the cops now think I staged it. Oh, what a tangled web we weave...*

"Didn't know her?" Corrigan says and raises a brow.

"All I know about Lisette Kingston is what I read in the newspapers. I didn't know her; never met her in my life."

"So, why did you kill her?"

"I didn't!" I protest. "What motive would I have?"

"Come on, Donovan, stand up." Corrigan demands. "You're going back to Coral Cove with us."

Corrigan cuffs me but, before we move toward the door, I ask, "Wait! Can I make a phone call?"

"Sure—after you're booked."

THE FOUR HOUR trip back to Coral Cove is uneventful. I remain silent and just stare out of the cruiser window. The arresting officers also remain silent. When we reach police headquarters, I'm taken into an interrogation room where Corrigan begins to question me after reading me my rights.

"Okay, Pal, why'd you do it?"

I'm so confused, all I can manage to say is, "I didn't kill her."

"Come on, kid, your story doesn't square with the evidence. We just want the truth."

"But, I *am* telling you the truth...*What evidence could they possibly have that I killed Kingston. Maybe I should confess to plagiarizing Prescott's novel if this is going to evolve into a murder charge.*

"Sure, sure. That's what they all say," Corrigan responds.

I detect skepticism in his voice when he utters the old familiar cliché and drop my head into my hands, covering my face. I'm barely able to grasp what is happening. *How did I come to this...this...this nightmare?* "I want a lawyer," I finally say.

I'm cuffed to a metal ring embedded in the steel table in a dank, smelly interrogation room. I ache from head to foot after the four hour ride from the Keys with my hands cuffed behind my back. Corrigan, my interrogator, looks up at the officer standing beside me. "Let him make the call then book him, Jackson, murder one."

Corrigan slams closed the notebook that had been laying open between us on the table. It is tabbed Kingston, Lisette — D.O.B. 06/26/68. Murder Investigation. He noisily scoots his chair back and stands, tucking the notebook under his arm. With his right forefinger, he lifts his windbreaker from the back of the chair and drapes it over his shoulder. "I'm going home."

"WAIT!" I shout. "You don't understand..."

"Tell it to the judge, Donovan, maybe he'll be more 'understanding.'" Corrigan is at the door in two strides, but before he exits, he turns and says, "I gave you a chance to come clean. I'm done with you."

As the door slams shut behind him, so does any hope I have of ever convincing anyone of what really happened. If I hadn't lived it, I wouldn't believe it either.

I USE MY single phone call privilege to contact my parents. When I tell them of my plight and tomorrow's court appearance, Dad says, "I'll call Fitzgerald as soon as we hang up. Even though he's our corporate lawyer, he knows who the best and brightest criminal law lawyers are." I detect sadness in Dad's voice as he continues, "I know you didn't commit murder, Son." He must have covered the mouthpiece as I can barely hear what he says to Mom, then he's back on the line. "We'll call and find out the time of your court appearance and be there and attempt to obtain your release."

"Thank you," is all I can say without completely breaking down.

"Stay strong, Son. We'll see you tomorrow."

WITHIN THE HOUR, Lorenzo "Lou" Penwell appears at the Dade County Detention Facility asking to see me. When he's ushered into my cell, he hands me his business card. I note that he is the lead partner in the law firm of Penwell, Sterger & Graves. I'm surprised that he would appear in person rather than sending an associate to do the preliminary interview. *Dad's influence?*

"Good evening, Mr. Donovan," Penwell says.

"And to you, Mr. Penwell," I reply. I'm so elated by the appearance of what I consider my lifeline that I'm reluctant to let go of his hand as we exchange greetings.

His smile is genuine and warm as he says, "Since we're going to be spending a lot of time together, please, call me Lou."

"Yes, sir. And I'm known as Cam."

Penwell nods and then sits down on the edge of my miserable cot. "Well, Cam, now that we've dispensed with the formalities, what is it that has precipitated the first degree murder charge?" he asks as he places a leather-bound notebook on his crossed legs and looks up at me, pen in hand.

I sit down next to him. "Well, I guess that is my quandary as well. My thought is that the plot in my first published novel mirrors that of an unsolved murder."

"Yes, that appears to be the rumor that is being circulated. My question is whether the plot in *Jeopardy*, which I am about to read, was based on the Lisette Kingston murder case that has been so highly publicized."

I run my hands through my hair. *Should I tell him of the plagiarism? He'll no doubt, find out sooner or later anyway. After all, he is my lawyer and is entitled to know. Besides, I don't want him to distrust me and if I hedge, that may shoot my credibility in the head.* I bite the bullet and tell him the full story from the day I accepted the internship to the present, including Prescott's drowning and Nikki's and my suspicions that Prescott killed Kingston. I conclude by confessing that I plagiarized Prescott's novel. "*Jeopardy* is a name I substituted for *Beguiled,* an unpublished novel written by Prescott. I was familiar with the novel because I formulated the manuscript along with doing some research that Prescott incorporated in the novel. I guess you might say I helped make it what it is and was satisfied with my role as a water boy of sorts. That is until Prescott drowned. Then I convinced myself that passing the novel off as my own harmed no one—especially not Prescott since he would never know the difference. I guess I considered taking credit for the novel was my way to exact my perceived pound of flesh for putting up with the demeaning way he treated me."

Penwell clears his throat, then speaks, "I must say, that's quite the story, Cam..."

I'm already on aggravation overload and I blurt, "It's *not* a story! It's the truth."

"Easy, Son, I didn't mean to imply you were lying. I'm just amazed at the bizarre sequence of events that led up to your arrest."

"Sorry," I murmer. "I guess my nerves are shot to hell and back."

"I appreciate your candor. Understand that what you tell me is a privileged communication—something I can't repeat without your permission. It is important to effective representation that an attorney's client tells him everything, and I mean *everything!* In other words, if you lead me down the wrong path, it is you who will suffer the consequences."

I nod.

Penwell then begins to page through his notes. "I see your friend, Nikki Palmer, was involved in most of the activities you related to me. Is that correct?"

"Yes, Nikki and I both transcribed for Prescott at one time or another. We spent a lot of time together that is until I moved back to the Keys."

"Right," Penwell says and checks his notes. "Tell me again how it was that you and Nikki determined that Prescott was Lisette Kingston's killer."

I stand and begin to pace the cell as I reflect on the series of events. "Well, that day, we shared our individual encounters with Prescott. Nikki was still tormented by Prescott's rage the evening he returned home from the book signing. We deduced the 'novice' he accused of having criticized him that night at the bookstore must have been Lisette Kingston and especially after we discussed his nonchalant attitude about Kingston's murder when he read the newspaper account aloud the next day."

Penwell continues to take notes as I add, "However, Nikki, trying to cut Prescott some slack, said that perhaps he had run out of plots and, in his desperation to get another novel published, decided to use a real murder and then incorporate it, in this case Kingston's, into the plot."

Penwell looks up from his writing. "Reasonable deduction," he says. "Nikki may very well be our best witness. That's assuming, of course, we can locate her."

"I think she still lives here in Coral Cove. Unfortunately, I haven't seen or talked to her in several years." I'm suddenly embarrassed by how I treated Nikki and uncertain as to her whereabouts and what her reaction will be upon being contacted.

Apparently sensing my discomfort, Penwell puts a calming hand on my shoulder and says, "It's okay, son, we'll find her. In the next day or two, Malcom Wendland, an investigator from our office, will be contacting you for leads and also for a more extensive interview."

Penwell closes his notebook and stands. As he reaches the door of the cell, he turns and with a puzzled look, asks, "Did the plot of the novel include details of the murder that were not in the newspapers or otherwise common knowledge?"

"Not that I know of," I respond realizing that if that were the case, it would be easy for the authorities to connect me to Lisette Kingston's murder—especially if they thought I was the author.

"By passing the novel off as your own, you in essence are responsible for its contents. If, and I say if, the novel not only mirrors what facts have been made public but facts that have been withheld, for whatever reason, the finger of guilt points squarely in your direction."

"Does that mean that I will have to prove I was not the author of *Jeopardy?* I thought I was innocent until proven guilty."

"Knowledge of non-publicized facts surrounding the murder is considered circumstantial evidence. In other words, facts known only to the killer and the law enforcement community leads to only one conclusion. Since you were not and are not a member of the law enforcement community, and, therefore, not privy to the information, the only way you would have such knowledge is as the killer."

"How plagiarism morphs into first degree murder is something I have pondered since my arrest. After speaking with you, I can see that it is not as absurd as I first thought. So, what you're telling me is that, if in fact, the novel contains non-public information about Lisette Kingston's murder, I will need to prove I was not the author."

"I'm afraid so. Appears that by doing so, you will, in essence, be admitting you are a plagiarist. Compared to the penalty for first degree murder, it is inconsequential."

"What *is* the penalty for first degree murder in Florida?"

"The mandatory sentence is either death or life without parole." I cringe. "And the penalty for plagiarism?" I ask.

"Most cases of plagiarism are civil in nature and result in an infringement action being brought by the owner of the plagiarized work. Here, the heir or heirs of Ashland Prescott. Under certain state and federal laws it can be a crime. Usually, it is considered a misdemeanor. If for example the plagiarist earns more than $2,500 from copyrighted material it can be a felony and the offender can face a fine of up to $250,000 and up to ten years imprisonment."

"But Prescott's novel was never copyrighted." I hastily add, hoping I'm home free.

"Remember from the media law class I presume you have taken, that a 'copyright' arises automatically upon creation provided it is an original expression and is in a fixed tangible form?"

"I do now" I say embarrassed by my lapse of recall and remembering that although it is recommended the work be registered, it is not required.

"Right now, our major concern is the first degree murder charge. It's obvious the authorities are not aware someone else wrote the novel forming the basis of the murder prosecution. Once we raise the defense that *Jeopardy* was not your original work, we will face the plagiarism issue. Until then, we need to concentrate on getting you released on bond."

"How much do you think that'll be?"

"Not so fast. Oftentimes, when the proof is evident and the presumption great, the prosecuting attorney will oppose bond. Otherwise, the bond schedule for a first degree murder charge is $1,000,000."

I stagger and grab hold of the bars on my cell for support. "$1,000,000?" I stammer, "I assume...if I can't raise it...I will rot in prison."

"There are various ways to arrange for a bond. Sometimes a bail bondsman posts the bond upon receiving a fee of 10% and security of some sort for the full bond. It is seldom a defendant has a million dollars sitting in a savings account somewhere. Although we will try, it is doubtful we can get the bond reduced."

"Great!" I say looking around my cell wondering if I can maintain my sanity long enough to endure the anxiety that is already consuming me.

"By the way, I'll already be in Judge Remington's courtroom when you arrive," Penwell says. "I have several matters on the docket in addition to your 'first appearance.'"

I issue a sigh of relief. By the way Penwell handles himself, I'm delighted with having him as my attorney. Since he has said nothing about fees, I ask, "Has my father already made the necessary financial arrangements?"

"Yes," he replies. "All that has been taken care of. As a matter of fact, both he and your mother will be present in court tomorrow. I plan to call your father as a witness in requesting a bond reduction."

"I thought you said it was unlikely the bond would be reduced."

"I did," Penwell says. "However, I have a Plan B."

I don't know how to interpret his broad smile.

AS I'M USHERED into the courtroom by two uniformed officers, I see Penwell seated at the defense table presumably with one of his clients. Out of the corner of my eye I spot my mother and father in the front row of the spectator section. Both manage a smile and a slight wave of the hand as I am led past.

Although no cameras have been allowed in the courtroom, I notice the press corps is there in full force with pens and press pads at the ready. Several turn and whisper to each other when they spot me.

After Penwell finishes with the hearing in progress, my case is called. Penwell succeeds in having the presiding judge, who is an imposing figure of a man with a silver white beard matching his full head of hair, authorize the removal of my handcuffs. An engraved nameplate perched on the front edge of His Honor's bench reads, "Rolland R. Remington, Circuit Court Judge." I watch as the judge alternates his gold rimmed glasses off and on the bridge of his nose depending on whether he is reading, listening or talking. Can't see any teeth because he never smiles.

"Are you Cameron Louis Donovan?" Judge Remington asks as I am accompanied to the podium by Penwell.

"I...I am," I stammer, frightened out of my wits and embarrassed by my predicament. The jail orange jump suit doesn't bolster my confidence nor do the laceless tennis shoes I'm wearing. If I could find a rock to hide under, I would.

"Mr. Donovan, you are here for what is called 'a first appearance.' That means that I will formally advise you of the nature of the charge filed against you, the possible penalties upon conviction and your rights. Do you understand that?"

"Yes, Your Honor."

"I see that Mr. Penwell has filed his formal appearance and the record will reflect he is present in court. He has also filed a motion to have bond set in your case. And in the event I determine that the proof of your guilt is evident and the presumption great, the law prevents me from allowing your release. Otherwise, I will be determining the amount of the bond. I will be doing so today. Do you likewise understand what I have just said?"

"Yes, Your Honor," I reply. "I was told that by my attorney." Judge Remington's demeanor is not as imposing and intimidating as his looks. The tone and manner of his speech has a calming effect.

Since I was arrested with a warrant, I already know the nature of the charge. He reads the charge anyway. In essence, I have been charged with the deliberate and premeditated murder of Lisette Kingston.

"Do you understand the nature of the charge brought against you?" Judge Remington asks as he removes his glasses and dangles them in front of him.

"Yes, Your Honor," I reply.

"In the event of a conviction and the jury recommends the death penalty, that is what you will, in all likelihood, receive. Do you understand that?"

"Yes, Your Honor," I again reply.

"Otherwise, upon conviction, I will be required to impose a sentence of life imprisonment without the possibility of parole. Do you understand the possible penalties?"

"Yes, Your Honor." Even though I understand what is being related to me, I don't quite understand how plagiarism translates into a capital offense. From an act of indiscretion to deliberate and premeditated murder certainly was not something I considered as a byproduct of plagiarism.

When the prosecuting attorney, F. Huffington Cromwell, was asked if he opposed the setting of bond, he answers "No."

"I take it your office is not contending the proof of guilt, in this case, is evident and the presumption great. Is that a correct assumption, Mr. Cromwell?"

"It is," Cromwell replies.

"Very well then, Mr. Penwell, is the defense able to advance any cogent reasons why the court should not follow the bond schedule in this case." Removing his glasses and raising his eyebrows, Judge Remington fixes his gaze on Penwell.

Penwell walks to the podium and, with the confidence of a seasoned attorney, addresses the court. "Your Honor," he begins, "the defendant, upon his arrest, was told by the arresting officers that he was being arrested for the murder of one Lisette Kingston because the plot in his bestselling novel, *Jeopardy*, mirrored that of the aforesaid murder. As you recall, that highly publicized murder case remained unsolved for several years—that is, until Mr. Donovan's novel was released."

At this point, Judge Remington interrupts. "Excuse me, Mr. Penwell, are you telling this court your client, a noted author, has been arrested because the murder plot in his novel, *Jeopardy,* mimics that of the Lisette Kingston murder."

"I am," Penwell replies.

Removing his glasses and placing them firmly on the top of his bench and, glaring in Cromwell's direction, Judge Remington asks in a harsh tone, "Mr. Cromwell, is what Mr. Penwell asserts indeed a fact?"

Cromwell, now standing, and blushing like a child caught with his hand in the proverbial cookie jar, stammers, "Partly, Your Honor. However, the defendant's novel contains information that was not released to the general public—information that only the killer would know."

Judge Remington clears his throat and still obviously irritated, asks, "Mr. Cromwell, it's not unusual for an author to base a so-called 'work of fiction' on an actual case, is it?"

"No, Your Honor, but..."

"And don't you suppose it is just as common for a novelist to invest some time investigating and interviewing witnesses connected with the case to create a believable plot and in the process, uncover information not generally known to the public or reported by the media?"

"Yes, but..."

"In fact, it's not uncommon for an author in a work of fiction to take literary license and embellish, is it, Mr. Cromwell?"

"No, Your Honor, but the defendant in our case would have to have been incredibly lucky or a clairvoyant to have known about the non-publicized evidence found at the scene of Lisette Kingston's murder."

"Are there any eyewitnesses to the murder that you or your office is aware of, Mr. Cromwell?" Judge Remington asks.

"None that we know of at this time," Cromwell says, as he slowly lowers himself into his chair.

Judge Remington adjusts his glasses and leafs through the file before him. Then, turning to my attorney, he asks, "Mr. Penwell, to cut to the chase, does your client have a criminal record?"

Penwell stands and putting a hand on my shoulder, says, "He has an unblemished record, is a budding author, lives in Key West not far from where his parents reside and is otherwise a reliable and responsible citizen."

Scanning the front row of the spectators' section of the courtroom and focusing on my parents, Judge Remington asks, "Sir and Madam, are you the parents of the defendant in this case?"

Both of my parents rise and nod their heads.

Judge Remington furrows his brow and looking sternly at my parents, asks, "If the court grants bond in this case and releases your son into your care and custody, meaning that, if he isn't already living with you he immediately will be and that you will insure that he makes any future court appearances?"

"We will," my father says and my mother vigorously nods agreement.

"In light of the unusual charges in this case, as well as the unusual circumstances, the court will deviate from the bond schedule and set a cash only bond at $250,000."

"Will your client be able to post such a bond?" Judge Remington asks Penwell.

"His parents are prepared to post the bond," Penwell says smiling back at my parents and then to me. While Judge Remington completes the bond authorization form and signs it, Penwell whispers, "Your parents were prepared to post the full $1,000,000. That was my 'Plan B'!"

BACK IN MY cell waiting for my release to be processed, I observe three guards huddled together. Loud enough for me to hear, one of the guards says, "Poor little rich kid." The second one says, "Didn't, wouldn't, couldn't and shouldn't," apparently referring to the shifting of blame by the privileged. The third, cupping his mouth with his hands, shouts, "Assert the *affluency* defense, kid; it beats the *insanity* defense every time."

I don't react; why start a fracas? I'll soon be on the outside where I can enjoy fresh air and blue skies. *So what if my parents can afford to bail me out. Anything is better than being locked in a human-sized birdcage.*

ON THE LONG drive to Key West I enjoy the light of day and wouldn't trade even this overcast morning for the artificial light of my dark, dank cell. Freedom is something I always took for granted. Now I know what my father meant when he said, "You don't know what you have until you lose it." Another one of his aphorisms comes to mind, "Savor the moment as it could be your last."

"You're awfully quiet back there," my father says.

"Probably planning the plot for the next novel," my mother offers.

I don't know quite how to level with my parents. My instinct tells me to reveal all. Without giving myself time to reconsider, I blurt, "I'm a fraud."

"Cam, what in the world are you saying?" my mother asks.

"I'm a fraud, Mom. Plain and simple, I'm a fraud."

"You're no such thing," my mother says as she unfastens her seatbelt and peers at me through the opening between the two front seats.

I move closer to the driver's side of the backseat and lean forward so that our heads are only inches apart. "I'm a thief and a liar," I say emphatically. "I stole someone else's work product, namely Prescott's novel, changed its name and pawned it off as my own. *Jeopardy* was not my creation but Prescott's. I lied about it being mine."

Whether out of relief, self-contempt, mortification or all three, I bury my head in my hands and sob like a child whose pet has just been run over by a passing vehicle.

"There, there," my mother says as she strains to put a calming hand on my head. "Don't be so hard on yourself. We love you no matter what."

"You don't understand," I stammer. "My career is ruined not to mention my reputation and ego."

"After the darkest hours there is the bright sun of day," my father says. "Think of it this way. If Lisette Kingston's killer wrote the offending novel and the author was not you, then you are off the hook. To reveal you are not the author is to proclaim your innocence." He then glances at me in the rearview mirror. "Kapish?"

After a long silence, my father asks, "Do you have any idea what law enforcement and the killer knew that no one else knew?"

"The death scene was written by Prescott just before I left Coral Cove to be with you and Mom immediately following your heart attack. Nikki transcribed it in my absence but showed me Prescott's handwritten text upon my return. She was upset with the graphic nature of the crime and Prescott's sadistic approach. I recognized it immediately as the depiction of Lisette Kingston's murder as reported in the local newspaper."

I pause and reflect on that moment when the realization set in that Prescott had staged a murder to provide fodder for his current murder mystery. *Case of a murder mystery writer gone mad or a matter of vengeance or a large dose of both?*

"You're shaking your head," my father says as he glances again at me in the rearview mirror. Mom cautions him to keep his eyes on the road. "The traffic is heavy this time of the day," she warns.

"I was just thinking of the vivid and realistic portrayal of the horror on the face of Prescott's *fictitious* victim. I'm sure it mirrored the real thing. It sends shivers down my spine just thinking about it."

I watch as Dad shakes his head no doubt sharing my disgust.

"At the time, I realized Prescott's script deviated somewhat from the newspaper accounts but not to any great extent. Fiction by its very nature is unrestrained and the object of fantasy. The victim in Prescott's novel having knocked over a canister of flour during the death struggle is the only major discrepancy I remember noting. Don't suppose that's what the prosecution is hanging its hat on, do you?"

"Prescott would have been 'incredibly lucky or a clairvoyant' to have known about something that unusual," Dad says. "Wasn't that what the prosecutor said this morning in court about the killer?"

"It was," I agree. "It is a stretch to say it was a lucky guess or that Prescott was clairvoyant. Without even knowing whether or not it was accurate, both Nikki and I knew in our hearts' Prescott was the killer."

"When you discussed Prescott's drowning," Dad interjects, "you hinted that Prescott knew about yours and Nikki's suspicions and may have taken you on that victory voyage to silence the two of you. Yet you didn't elaborate. Hopefully, that is something you have or will discuss with your attorney."

"Since it is an integral part of our defense, Mr. Penwell has instructed me, for the time being, to only discuss it with him."

"But, we're your parents," Mom protests.

"I make you witnesses by telling you about it. You'll find out in due time. Trust me."

TWO DAYS LATER, we're back in court. It's the arraignment. I enter a "not guilty" plea to the first degree murder charge. Penwell has also prompted me to ask for a jury trial. As we walked into court, Penwell was handed the discovery documents that the prosecution is required to provide. They consist of the police reports, witness interviews, witness and evidence lists and copies of everything in the possession of the prosecution. It does not include the prosecution's work product (internal notes, trial preparation or research) which is considered privileged. It is not long before we know the spilled canister of flour is the nail in the coffin. "If the author is the killer, then all we have to do is convince a jury you are not the author," Penwell says.

WHEN NIKKI RETURNS home from Hawaii, she sorts through the accumulated mail and the back issues of the *Coral Chronical*. The front page headline in one of the back issues of the newspaper catches her eye. It reads: *BEST-SELLING AUTHOR, CAMERON DONOVAN, RELEASED ON BAIL*. Nikki is stunned as she reads the lead article.

> Best-selling author, Cameron Donovan, was released on $250,000 bond today by Judge Rolland R. Remington. Donovan is charged with first degree murder in the death of Lisette Kingston, a long-time resident of Coral Cove.
>
> Arraignment has been set for Wednesday at 9:00 a.m. Donovan's attorney, the well-known Lorenzo "Lou" Penwell said his client will be entering a not guilty plea at that time.
>
> In jail garb and handcuffs, the accused looked less like a notable author of the bestselling novel, *Jeopardy*, than an alleged killer facing the death penalty. *Jeopardy* is a murder mystery mirroring the evidence found at the scene of the brutal murder of long-time resident Lisette Kingston. According to State Attorney F. Huffington Cromwell, *Jeopardy* deviated little in its plot from that of the mimicked murder. "In fact," Cromwell advised the court, "it contains information that had not been made public—information only the killer would know."

"I should have known *Jeopardy* was Prescott's *Beguiled*," Nikki said as she set aside the newspaper. *How stupid of me not to know. For a first-time author to have a best seller right out of the shoot is nothing less than miraculous. To boycott Cam for having dumped me by not purchasing his novel prevented me from becoming aware of his deception. Now I know why he has been avoiding me.*

In some ways, I'm relieved at learning of Cam's real reason for dumping me. To be exposed as a fraud would be far worse than avoiding me altogether. Maybe he surmised, and rightly so, that once I found out about the hoax it would be me who would be dumping him. I never dreamed Cam was capable of plagiarism. I do know, however, that Cam did not kill Lisette Kingston.

"MR. PENWELL, I have a Nikki Palmer on the phone. She insists on talking to you personally."

Penwell drops his pen on the yellow legal pad he had been making notes on and instructs the receptionist to put the call through immediately.

"Hello, Miss Palmer..."

"Yes. I'm calling for a number of reasons. First, I have received several business cards from an investigator named Malcom Wendland who apparently is affiliated with your firm. They were left with my father with instructions for me to call him. Unfortunately, I've been out of town and unable to respond."

"Understandable," Penwell replies.

"Secondly, I was a friend of your client, Cameron Donovan, and intimately familiar with the novel forming the basis of his criminal prosecution. Thirdly, and most importantly, I can categorically vouch for the fact that Cam did not author the novel and, therefore, is not Lisette Kingston's murderer."

"How soon can you be in my office?" Penwell anxiously asks.

"In less than half an hour," Nikki replies.

"I'll instruct the receptionist to escort you right in."

AS NIKKI IS ushered into Penwell's office, Penwell is surprised at how stunning Nikki is and how poised and confident she appears. He questions Cam's decision to trade fame for a flame.

Penwell points to two chairs positioned in front of his desk, motioning for Nikki to take one. "Please, call me Lou."

Nikki nervously poises herself on the edge of one of the chairs and stashes her purse under it. Taking a deep breath, she then says, "Mr. Penwell, I mean Lou, I must first inform you that I'm an ex-friend of Cam's. I'm here only because...only because it's the right thing to do."

"I understand that," Penwell says as he looks into Nikki's eyes. "Cam said that might be the case. But knowing I would be interviewing you, he also confided in me some of his personal feelings and asked me to convey them to you since he's not in a position to do so himself."

Nikki looks up with questioning eyes. "What did he want you to tell me?" she asks.

Penwell clears his throat and in a softer voice, says, "Cam told me that he had fallen in love with you. However, when he decided to plagiarize Prescott's novel he felt he had to give you up. He said it was one of the most difficult things he has ever had to do. His reasoning was that you were the only other person that knew what the novel was about and that, if you detected his plagiarism, you would not want to be with him anyway."

Nikki reaches into her purse for a tissue when tears begin to run down her cheeks. "What else did he say," she whispers.

Penwell rears back in his chair and clasps his hands across his chest, "He said he thought by breaking off with you completely, you would soon forget him." After a pause, Penwell adds, "Rest assured, my dear, he hasn't forgotten you."

Nikki nods, brushing tears from her cheeks.

Penwell leans forward and tents his fingers before him on his desk. He says, "Nikki, Cam rationalized that he would never have another opportunity such as the one presented to him by Prescott's death. He was overcome with an irresistible urge to plagiarize the novel and unfortunately, he caved in."

"But..." Nikki whispers, "as you so eloquently put it, he probably rationalized that there'll always be another girl. Right?"

"I, of course, cannot speak to that. However, it's only fair that you understand his frame of mind when all of this happened and I'm only telling you this at his request. Otherwise, anything that transpired between Cam and me would fall under the umbrella of attorney/client privilege and it would be unethical for me to reveal any of my conversation with him to you."

Nikki nods. "I just wanted some answers so I can close this episode and get on with my life. Thank you. What you told me helps."

"I understand your dilemma and I hope by revealing what Cam asked me to reveal, your pain has eased somewhat." After a moment, Penwell says, "Now I need some information from you."

"Okay," Nikki says and tucks the tissue into her purse.

"Among other things, Cam asserts that *you* transcribed the murder scene in *Beguiled* shortly after it was penned by Prescott. Is that correct?"

"Yes. Cam had to return home to the Keys because his father had a heart attack and his mother needed him. Actually, that's the only chapter that I typed in *Beguiled*."

"Do you remember the details of the murder scene?"

"Yes. In fact, I think I still have the original handwritten pages. I kept them to show Cam when he returned from the Keys since the scene more or less confirmed our suspicions regarding Prescott. Prescott must have forgotten that I hadn't returned the handwritten pages with the typewritten ones. He didn't ask where they were." Nikki looks thoughtful for a few moments, then adds, "Since Cam and I suspected Prescott killed Kingston, I think that's why I kept the handwritten pages."

"Are you sure you still have them?" Penwell asks with a hint of excitement in his voice.

"Pretty sure. I remember stashing them away with my school stuff at the end of the semester."

"Nikki, this is important. Those handwritten pages may very well be the evidence we need to prove Cam's innocence. As soon as you return home, would you please check to ensure that you still have them? If so, I'll need to take possession of them in order to disclose them to the DA and, of course, introduce them into evidence at trial."

"Sure. It must have been a sixth sense that I kept them. In my mind they were the 'smoking gun' to tie Prescott to the murder of Lisette Kingston."

Penwell nods as he removes his glasses and rubs his eyes. He then asks, "Have you read *Jeopardy?*"

"No." Nikki pauses briefly and looks down. She then adds, "When it was released, I, of course, didn't suspect it was Prescott's novel. And, I didn't want to give Cam the satisfaction of reading his 'great American novel.'"

"Great American novel?" Penwell asks.

"Yes. That's how he referred to the novel *he* was going to write."

"I see," Penwell mutters, then says, "I'm going to need your testimony at the preliminary hearing and then, provided the case is bound over for trial, at the trial itself." Penwell pauses a moment, "Will you testify as a cooperative witness?"

"Yes, of course, even though I'm still stinging from the way Cam dumped me, at least I now understand why. I would have testified under any circumstances, if for no other reason than it's the right thing to do. I absolutely know for certain Cam didn't kill Kingston and to let him die or spend the rest of his life in prison would be an unforgivable sin on my part."

Penwell nods. "While you're here, would you mind giving a formal statement to Malcom Wendland, my investigator. When I received your call, I alerted Mel. He's expecting you."

After Mel took Nikki's statement, he came into Penwell's office shaking his head.

"What's the matter, Mel?"

"Despite being jilted, Nikki is still willing to jump in turbulent waters to rescue a friend."

"For Cam, this will be the second time."

"Reminds me of the once popular song, *The Second Time Around*," Mel says.

"Or the song, *What Kind of Fool Am I?*" Penwell says and arches his eyebrows.

11

COURT OF INQUIRY

At Penwell's urging, I waive the preliminary hearing. "We gain little by going through the motions. We already know the prosecution's theory of the case mainly through the discovery the prosecution is required by law to provide. To them, our theory is still a mystery. Why alert them to the defense and give them time to counter?" Penwell looks at me for a response.

"Mel has briefed me on preliminary hearings and their benefits and detriments," I say.

"So you're familiar with the cost-benefit analysis approach?"

"My college courses prepared me well."

"And with regard to the cost benefits of waiving the preliminary hearing, what say you?"

"Since the preliminary hearing is only concerned with whether or not there is probable cause or reasonable grounds to believe I committed a crime, and not proof beyond a reasonable doubt as in trial, it is inevitable the charge will not be dismissed but bound over for trial."

"Right you are!" Penwell says. "And do the benefits of waiving the preliminary hearing outweigh the detriments?" he asks.

"By the prosecution agreeing to waive the death penalty in exchange for us waiving the preliminary hearing, it appears to be a fair exchange."

When my father and mother are brought into Penwell's office and told about the proposed agreement with the prosecution and their willingness to waive the death penalty, my father asks, "Why? What do they have to gain by doing so?"

"The prosecution already knows they have a weak case," Penwell responds. "By conceding that the 'proof was *not* evident and the presumption *not* great' at the bond hearing, they exposed their apprehension. And the grilling foisted on Cromwell at the hearing by Judge Remington took some of the wind out of their sails. In other words, their confidence has been shaken and getting the case bound over for trial does not appear to be such a slam-dunk after all."

My father smiles at Penwell apparently satisfied with the explanation. Knowing that the death penalty is no longer a consideration eases the situation and makes the ordeal a little more bearable—not just for me but my parents as well. It also takes some of the pressure away from Penwell. Without the deal, a guilty verdict would trigger the death penalty. *Whew!*

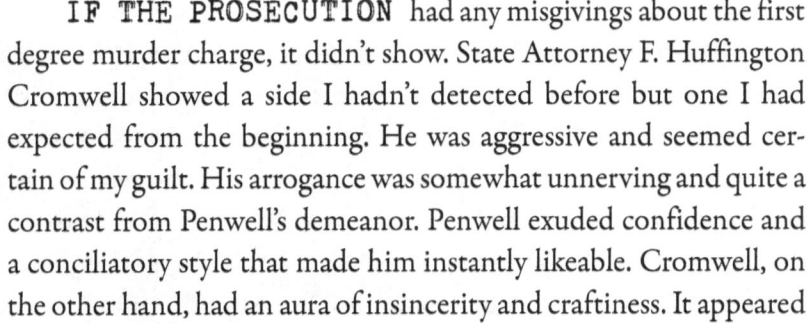

IF THE PROSECUTION had any misgivings about the first degree murder charge, it didn't show. State Attorney F. Huffington Cromwell showed a side I hadn't detected before but one I had expected from the beginning. He was aggressive and seemed certain of my guilt. His arrogance was somewhat unnerving and quite a contrast from Penwell's demeanor. Penwell exuded confidence and a conciliatory style that made him instantly likeable. Cromwell, on the other hand, had an aura of insincerity and craftiness. It appeared the prospective jurors didn't like him either.

Jury selection was cumbersome. Penwell said he could almost tell who he wanted on the jury without having to ask any questions. He said, however, his *voir dire* was designed more to inform the jury of our theory of the case than to probe into a juror's background and leanings though the latter was also important.

Though we debated who would be the most sympathetic and dispassionate, men or women, it made no difference in the last analysis. The jury, as impaneled, consisted of six of each. Virtually all were middle class of varying races and creeds. No professionals in the traditional sense or any educators were selected. For the most part they were nondescript and if they had biases towards authors or the media, none were readily apparent. The oldest juror was 64, and the youngest 22 and the rest somewhere in between. The same juror profile applied to the alternates. None had prior jury service. Like me, they were novices to the criminal justice system.

"Since the prosecution has the burden of proving an accused's guilt beyond a reasonable doubt, they go first and last," Penwell says. "We don't have to give an opening statement, but we will. We want them to know there are two sides to the story from the get-go."

"Ladies and Gentlemen of the jury," Cromwell begins. "All of us like to read a good novel. Mystery and intrigue seems to be one of the most popular genres. That and courtroom drama are my favorites.

"The determination of the best novels is market driven. In other words, the bestselling novels presumably are the ones most read. Being readership driven, every aspiring author wants to write 'the great American novel' which requires a unique and realistic or, what is sometimes called, believable plot. With the hundreds of thousands of novels competing with each other in the market place, unless a novel is truly outstanding, it will be lost in the mire.

"In his quest to create a realistic and believable plot, the defendant in this case, Cameron Donovan, set up his own murder scene by committing what was up to now, the perfect murder. In a novel he called *Jeopardy*, he was able to depict a scene so gruesome, grisly and graphic that the reader felt he or she was witnessing the actual murder. A kind of out-of-body experience, if you will, watching events unfold as they really happened.

"The evidence will show that the murder scene in *Jeopardy* mirrored that of the Lisette Kingston murder, a gruesome and sordid murder that appeared staged. The evidence will show that not all the facts surrounding the murder were made public. One of those facts known only to a select few law enforcement officers and to the killer, was an overturned canister that spilled its contents, to-wit: all-purpose flour over the counter and onto the floor. It was apparently knocked over during the death struggle. Who knocked it over only the killer and Ms. Kingston know. And Ms. Kingston is not here to tell you about it. However, the evidence survives and speaks for itself.

"Since only law enforcement and Lisette Kingston's murderer knew about the spilled canister of flour, then by the process of elimination, we can determine the source of that revelation. The evidence will show that that source was not law enforcement as they never made the information public. The evidence will also show that no outsiders were made privy to that information and that the defendant, Cameron Donovan, never was a member of the law enforcement community. That means Cameron Donovan was the killer!

"If the evidence presented during this trial is as outlined and as the prosecution anticipates, we will have no hesitation whatsoever at the conclusion of the trial in asking you to return a guilty verdict."

I'm troubled by the fact that many of the jurors are nodding as Cromwell makes his points and none are looking in my direction except for a furtive glance now and then.

"They think I'm guilty," I whisper to Penwell.

"They promised they would keep an open mind until they heard all the evidence," Penwell tells me. "It's not over 'til it's over," he adds.

"The prosecution," Penwell begins, "having the burden of proof, has outlined the facts they expect to prove in convincing you beyond a reasonable doubt that Cameron Donovan is guilty. Remember, their opening statement is not evidence. It is nothing more than the revelation in outline fashion of the facts they *expect* to prove.

"Although a defendant in an American courtroom is not required to prove his or her innocence and not required to testify, there is some expectation that he or she will attempt, in some fashion, to refute the various allegations and produce some evidence of their own.

"That having been said, the defense will concede that information regarding the overturned canister and the spilled flour found at the crime scene was known only by a select few and that in all likelihood the killer was the author of the original manuscript of what later was entitled *Jeopardy*. The evidence will show that the original manuscript was written by a local author, Ashland Prescott, not the defendant, Cameron Donovan."

Penwell could not have scripted the jurors' reaction any better. Even Judge Remington gasped. An exasperated Judge Remington banged his gavel repeatedly to regain order. "Any further outburst like that and I'll have the bailiff clear the courtroom," Judge Remington announced. To give the air a chance to clear, a recess was declared.

Turning to Penwell, I ask, "I thought you disclosed that fact to Cromwell."

"I did," Penwell responded. "He just laughed and said 'tell it to the jury.'"

After the recess, Penwell continued with his opening statement.

"As I said prior to the break, Cameron Donovan, the defendant in this case, was *not* the author of *Jeopardy* or its predecessor

Beguiled. An author known to all of you by the name of Ashland Prescott actually penned the death scene without any help from the defendant. Cameron Donovan was a mere scribe and intern for Ashland Prescott.

"When the actual death scene was penned, Cameron Donovan was actually out of town due to the hospitalization of his father. The person who transcribed Prescott's chapter detailing the death scene was a student and former typist employed by Prescott by the name of Nikki Palmer. Both Cameron Donovan and Nikki Palmer will be called as witnesses for the defense."

At this point, Judge Remington interrupted Penwell's opening statement and called both attorneys to the bench and outside the ears of the jury, had what appeared to be a heated discussion. Penwell later told me what transpired.

"Mr. Penwell, the gravamen of the first degree murder prosecution of your client is the revelation in his novel of non-public facts involving key evidence. The prosecution's contention appears to be that the author of that novel wouldn't have been privy to that evidence if he weren't the killer. If the charged defendant wasn't the author then it's unlikely he was the killer. My question to you Mr. Penwell is why you didn't disclose that fact to Mr. Cromwell so that we could have avoided wasting all the taxpayers' hard-earned money pursuing a frivolous prosecution?"

"I tried," Penwell replied. "Mr. Cromwell just looked at me and laughed as he said something to the effect of 'Go tell it to the jury.'"

Judge Remington then glared at Cromwell and asked, "Huffington, is that correct?"

"That the defendant is not the author is an absurd notion Mr. Penwell advances, Your Honor," Cromwell reportedly replied. "Prescott is not here to refute it nor is Ms. Kingston. I wouldn't believe the defendant on a stack of Bibles and who's to say this Miss Palmer isn't also a liar."

Judge Remington then sat back in his chair and folded his arms. Finally, leaning forward to avoid being overheard by the jury, he said, "Huff, I hope you know what you're doing." And to both attorneys he said, "Clearly this is a jury matter." And to Penwell, he said, "Proceed with your opening statement. But please move this thing along."

"I will, Your Honor," Penwell said and headed back to the podium.

"Ladies and Gentlemen of the jury, after you have heard all the evidence, you will come to the realization that, in all likelihood, the author of the death scene in *Jeopardy* and its predecessor *Beguiled* was Lisette Kingston's killer. But since the defendant is neither the author of the death scene or Lisette Kingston's killer, you will have no recourse but to return a not guilty verdict. Don't do it because I have asked you to do it, but because it is the right thing to do."

"The amount of evidence produced by the prosecution was meager considering it was a first degree murder prosecution," Penwell would say at the conclusion of the prosecution's case-in-chief. Even though I was not familiar with such prosecutions, I was of the same mind.

The key evidence presented by the prosecution consisted of a copy of *Jeopardy*. The death scene was read out loud to the jury and a police detective, who I recognized as Blake Corrigan, compared it to the investigative report. Both renditions, of course, contained a description of the overturned canister and the spilled flour. It was obvious that the death scene in the novel paralleled that of the actual death scene.

WHEN IT WAS the defense's turn to present evidence, I was the first witness called.

"Would you state for the record your full name and any nickname?" Penwell asked.

"My full name is Cameron Louis Donovan. I don't usually use my middle name. My friends call me 'Cam.'"

"What is your main occupation or profession?"

"I am a writer, a novelist to be exact."

"Do you possess a college degree?"

"Yes, I have a Master of Arts degree from Wellington York University in Ft. Lauderdale."

"What was your major?"

"I graduated with dual majors in English and Journalism."

"Did you have occasion to do an internship for a New York bestselling author by the name of Ashland Prescott?"

"Yes."

"Did you actually reside with Mr. Prescott during your internship?"

"Both the residence and our respective offices were in Prescott Mansion."

"In performing your duties as an intern, did you have occasion to work on a novel Mr. Prescott named *Beguiled*—the same one you later renamed *Jeopardy?*"

"Yes."

"Did you author any part of that novel?"

"No."

"What did you do?"

"I did some research as Mr. Prescott directed but mainly I transcribed his handwritten manuscript and formatted it in the form required by his publisher."

"Did you make any changes other than maybe correcting some spelling errors or punctuation?"

"From the beginning of my internship with Mr. Prescott, I was advised that my job description was as a *scribe,* not as an editor and that if I had any corrections, they were to be minor in nature. I was prohibited from adding, deleting or rephrasing anything."

"Now, you heard detectives from the Coral Cove Police Department testify as to the death scene in *Jeopardy,* the name you gave to the novel *Beguiled* written by Ashland Prescott, correct?"

"Yes."

"By the way, Cam, did you make any changes to the death scene or any other part of Mr. Prescott's novel, other than to rename the characters and the novel itself and, of course, add your name as the author, when you published *Jeopardy?*"

"No, other than rename the characters and novel and claim myself as the author, *Jeopardy* is identical to *Beguiled.*"

"Do you realize that by your sworn testimony here today you have admitted to being a plagiarist, that is, someone who has copied another's work, without the latter's consent, and passed it off as his own?"

"I'm ashamed to say that I do."

"So that we are all clear, Cam, is your testimony that you never wrote or penned the death scene that appears in *Jeopardy?*"

"It is!"

"Who authored the death scene?"

"Ashland Prescott."

"Did you write or direct the writing of the death scene?"

"No."

"Did you ever transcribe that portion of Mr. Prescott's novel?"

"It was transcribed by Mr. Prescott's former typist, Nikki Palmer."

"How was it that you weren't the transcriber of that part of the novel?"

"I was in Key West at the bedside of my father, who had just suffered a heart attack, and it just so happened that Nikki Palmer filled in for me."

"In what form would Mr. Prescott present the portions of the novel that were to be transcribed?"

"In the past he apparently dictated his novels. With all the interruptions, such as book signings, lectures, speeches, special events and so on, he began handwriting his novels and having them transcribed or should I say computerized. He didn't like the computer and at least during my internship, never used the computer. Instead, I would receive Mr. Prescott's handwritten submission on sheets torn from a yellow legal pad with the page number and the date on the upper left-hand corner."

"After the transcription, would you return Mr. Prescott's printed submissions along with the typewritten transcription?"

"Mr. Prescott was fussy about receiving both back so he could make sure the transcription was accurate. On the rare occasions I would forget to return his printed pages, he would come and retrieve them."

"As a result of your internship, did you become familiar with Mr. Prescott's handwriting?"

"Absolutely. I not only read what he had written but watched him write. He had a distinct style that I would recognize if I saw it again."

"Cam, I'm handing you what has been marked for identification as Defendant's Exhibit D-1, consisting of a number of legal-sized sheets with a frayed top bearing handwriting on the major portions thereof and the page number and date on the upper left-hand corner, and ask if you recognize it."

"I recognize the handwriting as that of Ashland Prescott including the page number and date on the upper left-hand corner of each page."

"Are you sure that the handwriting is that of Ashland Prescott?"
"Yes."

When Penwell retrieves Defendant's Exhibit D-1, he sets it back on the clerk's table. "Are you intending to offer that as an exhibit at this time?" Judge Remington asks.

"No, Your Honor," Penwell replies, "not until we establish its relevancy. And I will be doing that through another witness."

"Very well then, Mr. Penwell, you may continue with your witness."

"Cam, when was the first time you heard the name Lisette Kingston?"

"When Mr. Prescott read the newspaper account of the murder at the breakfast table the following morning."

"Did you know Lisette Kingston or ever meet her?"

"No!"

"Did you ever have any contact with her or she with you?"

"No."

"Did you kill Lisette Kingston?"

"No!"

It is now Cromwell's opportunity to cross-examine me. I'm somewhat apprehensive but confident that the time I spent with Penwell has prepared me well for the anticipated all-out assault. Since Detective Blake Corrigan is the prosecution's advisory witness sitting at the prosecution's table with Cromwell and convinced of my guilt, I know I'm in for a bumpy ride.

"With Ashland Prescott out of the picture," Cromwell began, "you feel fairly confident your testimony will not be contradicted, don't you, Mr. Donovan?"

"As my attorney advised me before coming to court, there is nothing to fear if I tell the truth. To answer your question, I am telling the truth and am, therefore, confident."

"You don't deny plagiarizing Ashland Prescott's work, do you?"

"No. Nor am I proud of what I did."

"If it weren't for being charged with the brutal murder of Lisette Kingston, you wouldn't be making that admission now, would you Mr. Donovan?"

"Ever since I claimed credit for the novel, it has gnawed at me. I'm not sure I could have stifled my regret too much longer."

"My point is this, Mr. Donovan. When it benefited you career-wise and economically, you lied about being the author of the novel detailing Lisette Kingston's murder, didn't you?"

"Yes."

"And, now facing a first degree murder charge, its expedient for you to again lie, lie to save your skin. Isn't that true?"

"I can see how my credibility might be called into question. However, being under oath and having corroborative evidence to back up my innocence, I can categorically tell you I'm not capable of murder and certainly not the one who killed Lisette Kingston. You're prosecuting the wrong person."

"You don't deny, do you, that the death scene in *Jeopardy* contains information that was not made public?"

"No, nor did Ashland Prescott's manuscript from which the death scene was mimicked."

"That is *your* contention?"

"Mine, and Defendant's Exhibit D-1 the handwritten notes of Ashland Prescott and the statements of our next witness."

"Your Honor, I move that the answer be stricken as non-responsive," Cromwell says obviously not pleased with the way the cross-examination is unfolding.

When Penwell rises to respond, Judge Remington motions for him to remain seated. "Mr. Cromwell," Judge Remington says in a firm voice, "Mr. Donovan is only answering your questions which, I might point out, are open-ended and don't call for a 'yes' or 'no' answer. If you want to orchestrate the answers, you need to rephrase your questions."

Flushed and no doubt embarrassed by the scolding, Cromwell tries to regain his composure by conferring with his advisory witness, Detective Blake Corrigan.

When he returns to the podium, he announces he has "no other questions." After I am excused and return to my seat, a recess is declared and in a hushed tone, Penwell turns to me and says, "Great job!"

"Easy when you're telling the truth," I reply.

———————— ≈ ————————

WHEN WE RECONVENE Nikki Palmer is called to the stand and is sworn in. She is all business and does not look in my direction. After Penwell asks for her name and address and Nikki responds, he spends little time before delving into the heart of the matter.

"Miss Palmer, are you acquainted with the death scene in Mr. Donovan's novel?"

"I am."

"When was the first time you were introduced to the death scene?"

"Right after Ashland Prescott wrote it."

"When was that?"

"A little over two years ago when I was filling in for Cam—or, ah...Cameron Donovan. Mr. Donovan had been called home when his father had suffered a heart attack and Mr. Prescott asked me to transcribe for him in Mr. Donovan's absence."

"What did the transcription consist of?"

"Several dozen handwritten pages torn from a yellow legal pad with the page numbers and date noted on the top left hand corner of each page."

"When you say 'handwritten,' who's handwriting was it?"

"Ashland Prescott's."

"How do you know?"

"I worked for Ashland Prescott as the transcriber of the manuscripts for his various novels for a whole school year and was familiar with his writing and the unique way he labeled each page."

"I hand you what is marked for identification as Defendant's Exhibit D-1 and ask that you examine each page."

Nikki sifts through the pages carefully examining each page. After she is finished, she looks up. For a brief moment our eyes meet.

"Miss Palmer, have you had ample time to examine that exhibit?"

"I have," she says, and continues to hold them in her lap.

"Have you seen those pages on any previous occasion?"

"I have."

"What are they?"

"They're the pages of the death scene in *Beguiled* that were hand-written by Ashland Prescott and given to me to be transcribed."

"How do you know they are one and the same?"

"I recognize the content, Mr. Prescott's handwriting and his notation in the upper left-hand corner of each of the pages."

"Are you positive they are the same?"

"The marks penciled in the various margins I made to remember the place I started and stopped."

"Other than the marks, are the documents the same ones handed you for transcription by Ashland Prescott during the time you substituted for Cameron Donovan, the defendant in this case?"

"One and the same."

"How is it you ended up with the custody and control of the documents you are holding? Didn't Mr. Prescott usually require his drafts be returned along with the transcription?"

"I kept them for Cam, I mean Mr. Donovan, to review and make comparisons with my transcription in the event he was required to do so by Mr. Prescott. I also kept them to show Mr. Donovan because I was alarmed by the contents. They were very graphic and so much unlike Mr. Prescott. To me, they appeared to be too much like the newspaper accounts of the Lisette Kingston murder. Mr. Prescott never asked for them back and I never returned them. I've had them ever since."

Addressing Judge Remington, Penwell says, "Your Honor, at this time we offer into evidence Defendant's Exhibit D-1."

"Any objection, Mr. Cromwell?" Judge Remington asks.

"Yes, Your Honor," Cromwell replies. "There's been no testimony from a handwriting expert to verify that the handwritten death scene contains the handwriting of Ashland Prescott. For all we know, anyone could have written it."

Again, when Penwell rises to respond, Judge Remington motions for him to remain seated. "Objection overruled. Lay witnesses, as you know Mr. Cromwell, are allowed to express opinions if they are familiar with the particular handwriting. Here, we have not just one but two lay witnesses identifying the handwriting." Judge Remington nods for Penwell to continue.

"Miss Palmer, I have just one last question. Who was the author of the death scene in *Jeopardy*?"

"Objection," Cromwell shouts.

"Overruled," Judge Remington announces.

"Would you like for me to repeat the question?" Penwell asks.

"Please!" Nikki responds.

"Who was the author of the death scene in *Jeopardy*?"

"Ashland Prescott!"

I can tell the jurors have been persuaded in my favor. For the first time in the trial, they don't appear to be afraid to make eye contact. In fact, from time-to-time, several smile at me.

When I relay my observations to Penwell, he states, "I've noticed the same thing. In their minds and up to now, contrary to the law, they've considered you guilty until proven innocent."

"Does that mean we've proven my innocence 'beyond a reasonable doubt'?"

"Means that they no longer consider you guilty."

"LADIES AND GENTLEMEN of the jury," Cromwell begins. "During the prosecution's opening statement, we told you that if the evidence produced at the trial was as we anticipated, we would have no difficulty in asking you to return a guilty verdict. Well, the evidence is as we anticipated and now we are asking you to find the defendant, Cameron Donovan, guilty of first degree murder in the brutal killing of Lisette Kingston.

"Relating a fact not made public in the death scene depicted in his bestselling novel, *Jeopardy*, the defendant, in essence, has confessed to the murder. Relating something known only to the killer and law enforcement means the insider, if not a member of the law enforcement community, must be the killer.

"For Cameron Donovan to have claimed all along to be the author of *Jeopardy* when it benefited him and now to disavow any connection other than being the transcriber, when it again benefits him, is to impugn the intelligence of you, the jurors. To be fooled once is understandable; to be fooled twice is not.

"When you recount the evidence, remember the death scene for the novel was written *after* the murder of Lisette Kingston. The unrefuted evidence is that the defendant helped Ashland Prescott with that novel. Who's to say the defendant didn't also help write the novel. After all, the defendant is a novelist. Recall, the defendant admitted to having done some of the research. Who's to say that research didn't include a reference to the overturned canister of flour?

"There's an old adage that comes to mind when I think of the evidence in this case. 'You live by the sword; you die by the sword.' To claim to be the author of a novel containing nonpublic information carries with it the consequences of that claim.

"Ladies and Gentlemen, the message you send by a guilty verdict in this case is: Mr. Donovan, 'you can fool some of the people some of the time but you can't fool all of the people all of the time.'

"The issue in this case involves credibility. If the defendant lied about being the author of the novel, including the death scene, isn't it just as likely he lied about not being Lisette Kingston's killer. If the defendant would steal someone else's work ostensibly for fame and fortune, wouldn't he likewise create the believable plot by stealing someone else's life?

"I have had the dubious distinction of prosecuting this case. My obligation is to see that you arrive at a fair and just verdict. That is the oath I took when I was first elected to this office. However, that obligation is fulfilled as I turn this case over to you Ladies and Gentlemen. In doing so, I ask that you return a fair and a just verdict. And a fair and just verdict in this case is a verdict of guilty. Thank you."

Penwell is not in a hurry to get to the podium. I surmise he is waiting for the dust to settle and rouse curiosity. Whatever the reason, all of the jurors' eyes are peeled on him and some are straining as he speaks.

"Ladies and Gentlemen, Mr. Cromwell is a magician much like Houdini conjuring up an illusion—in this case an illusion of guilt. Remember, emotion is not reason and rhetoric is not evidence. Your verdict must not be based on supposition but solely on the evidence presented at trial.

"When we boil the evidence down to its most common elements, we are left with the following:

1 - The defendant, Cameron Donovan, plagiarized an unpublished novel written by Ashland Prescott.

2 - Prescott's novel contained a death scene that mirrored that of an unsolved murder and included information that, excluding law enforcement, only the killer would know.

3 - The author of the death scene containing the nonpublic information was Ashland Prescott.

4 - Because the defendant, Cameron Donovan, was thought to be the author of the death scene, he was

arrested and charged with first degree murder in the unsolved murder case.

5 - The defendant, Cameron Donovan, had no connection to any facet of the unsolved murder other than having plagiarized the scene and included it in his own novel unedited.

"The prosecution's contention all along is that because the defendant's novel contained the aforementioned crime scene, he must be the killer. In other words, the author of the crime scene with the nonpublic information is obviously the killer. Open and shut case. Right? Wrong! Cameron Donovan was not the author. Plain and simple. How likely is it that a college student, who has never published anything, writes a best seller? Not being the author, Cameron Donovan is *not* the killer.

"One thing the prosecution and defense agree on is that the evidence speaks for itself. Remember the prosecution's opening statement to that effect. Defendant's Exhibit D-1 *is* the 'smoking gun.' It identifies the killer. And, the killer is not Cameron Donovan, the defendant in this case.

"The prosecution, in its zeal to solve Lisette Kingston's murder, sought to make an innocent man the scapegoat. Instead of conducting a thorough investigation, they relied on a work of fiction to solve a murder mystery. By arresting the author, they thought they had solved the crime. But now that the truth is known, we hope you will rectify the injustice by finding the defendant, Cameron Donovan, not guilty. Thank you."

MY PARENTS AND I hang around Penwell's office waiting for the jury to return with its verdict. Every time the phone rings, we think it is the call announcing that the jury has reached a verdict. No such luck. At 4:30 p.m., we are told by Penwell that he received the call. However, it was not with the news we had expected. "The jury is dead-locked and they have been released for the night to return to resume deliberation at 8:00 a.m. tomorrow," he announces.

"What happens if they can't reach a verdict?" Mom asks.

"Judge Remington will declare a mistrial and we start all over," Penwell replies.

"What do you think the hang-up is?" Dad asks. Without giving Penwell time to respond, he says, "Having sat through the whole trial, I find it a no-brainer."

"I never second-guess a jury," Penwell responds. "The ones you think you've won, you lose and the ones you think you lose, you win. Go figure!"

"Maybe they think I provided Prescott with the nonpublic information or maybe, because I lied about being the author, they think I also lied about not being the killer," I speculate out loud.

"Once your credibility is at issue, everything you say is scrutinized. I'm guessing the majority are for an acquittal and there are a few stubborn holdouts that take their duties seriously particularly in a murder prosecution. Hashing and rehashing the evidence sometimes takes days. Guess we have to be patient."

"What happens if they return a guilty verdict?" Mom asks.

"Judge Remington will revoke the bond and Cam will be returned to jail. In the interim, we would file an appeal and attempt to have him released on bond."

"And if Cam is acquitted?" Dad asks.

"The bond will be released and you will get your money back and, of course, Cam will once again be a free man."

"I pray that will be the case," Mom says.

BY 10:30 THE following day, we are told the jury has returned a verdict. I'm a bundle of nerves when I reach the courthouse. My parents and I are greeted by Penwell and ushered into the courtroom. Everything from that point is a blur. When the verdict is read, I'm not sure whether it is guilty or not guilty. I look at Penwell and frown. "What did he say?" I manage to mumble. With a wide grin, Penwell says, "Not guilty! You've been found not guilty!"

I'm so elated I can't speak. I feel weak and Penwell steadies me. "I can't believe it," I say as I'm now encircled by my parents. When it sinks in, I thank God, Penwell and my parents in that order. "We did it!" I say still trying to convince myself I've been exonerated.

By 11:00, my bond is exonerated and I'm a free man. When I leave the courtroom most of the jurors are waiting for me. They seem genuinely pleased with their verdict and encourage me to keep writing. One even asks me when my next book will be out. I sag when I reach our car. Apparently, in anticipation of a victory celebration, a lunch is waiting for us at Penwell's office. When we reach the library, we notice it has been decorated with party favors and are greeted by Penwell's staff.

"This was not a spur of the moment thing," Penwell's secretary says. "Virtually all of Mr. Penwell's cases end this way."

I was overcome by emotion when I thanked Penwell and bade him goodbye. "Your career is not ending; it's only beginning," he said. "You have a lot of catching up to do," he added and raised his eyebrows. I knew instantly that he was referring to Nikki.

TURBULENT WATERS

As Marjo Corrigan pours coffee into her husband's mug, she peers over his shoulder at the front page headlines of the newspaper he is holding. *AUTHOR FOUND NOT GUILTY.* Curious as to the newspaper account, she reads:

> Into the second day of deliberations in the murder prosecution of Cameron Donovan, the six man-six woman jury returned its verdict of not guilty in the highly publicized first degree murder case.

> In his bestselling novel, *Jeopardy*, Donovan was alleged to have detailed the murder scene in such a way as not only to duplicate the murder of long-time resident Lisette Kingston but presented facts that only the killer could have known. "It was too accurate and too unique to have been a coincidence," police detective Blake Corrigan told the Coral Chronicle shortly after the verdict was announced.

> During the trial, it was established that Donovan was not the author of the death scene but that it was penned by local bestselling author, Ashland

Prescott, for whom Donovan was an intern. In his interview with the Coral Chronicle, Donovan said, "By plagiarizing Prescott's novel, I crossed the line and by doing so jeopardized my career and my future credibility. If Prescott were alive, I would apologize to him and try to find a way to make it up to him."

Ashland Prescott was the author of four bestsellers and tragically lost at sea during a boating accident several years ago. He was known for his philanthropy as much as for his writing. He hired interns from the state's colleges and universities and is credited for having launched the careers of a number of writers, including Cameron Donovan.

"Looks like Donovan got away with another one!" Marjo tells her husband.

"What do you mean?" Corrigan asks.

"He doesn't have to answer for the death of Lisette Kingston and it appears he won't have to answer for the death of Ashland Prescott."

"You've been reading too many murder mysteries," Corrigan says as he peers over his glasses at Marjo.

"Think about it," she says as she pours coffee for herself. "If Prescott had survived the so-called accident, Donovan wouldn't have been able to pilfer Prescott's novel and make it appear to be his own. Donovan's only claim to fame is taking credit for a novel that was written by Prescott."

After careful reflection, Corrigan says, "By Jove, Marjo, you may be on to something. The only thing Donovan may have added to the novel is the reference to the canister of spilled flour which only the killer knew about. If he would steal Prescott's novel and lie about it, it is just as likely that he not only killed Lisette Kingston but Ashland Prescott as well."

"Wasn't the canister and flour reference first in Prescott's draft of the murder scene?" Marjo asks.

"At trial, it came out that Donovan not only transcribed Prescott's manuscript for *Beguiled,* but provided research as well. Undoubtedly, that research included material related to Lisette Kingston's murder scene. Donovan could very easily have included the reference to the overturned canister and spilled flour not realizing it was not public knowledge."

"Where is my cellphone?" Corrigan asks looking under the folded newspaper.

"On the counter where you left it," Marjo says and rises to retrieve it.

"Never mind," Corrigan says as he ambles to the kitchen counter and unplugs the charger.

"Who are you calling?" Marjo asks.

"Pat Mahoney. We have a staff meeting at 10:30 and I'll have him pull up the file on Prescott's drowning and include it on the agenda."

"What would you do without me?" Marjo asks.

"Be just an average cop," Corrigan says and both smile.

WHEN CORRIGAN ARRIVES at the Coral Cove Police Department, he is told the Prescott drowning investigative file has been placed on his desk.

As he begins leafing through the sparse pages, he is reminded that Nikki Palmer had been aboard *Best Seller IV* at the time of Ashland Prescott's accident. When he compares Palmer's statement with Donovan's, he scratches his head. *They're identical!*

"Mahoney, get in here!" Corrigan barks over the intercom.

"What did I do now?" Mahoney asks, then sarcastically adds, "Did you get a promotion?"

"If the CCPD knew what they were doing, I'd hold rank."

As Mahoney sits opposite Corrigan at the small conference table, Corrigan hands him the Prescott investigative file. "Here, look at the two reports. One was taken by Joseph Tanner and the other by Sam Cummings right after Prescott's drowning was reported."

After Mahoney reviews the two reports, which were taken by two different officers from two different witnesses who had been separated from each other, neither apparently hearing what the other had to say, he shakes his head. "The interview by Joseph Tanner of Nikki Palmer is the mirror image of Sam Cummings' interview of Cameron Donovan," Mahoney responds.

"My sentiments exactly!" Corrigan says. "What does that tell you?"

"It tells me their statements were coordinated and rehearsed and, no doubt, fabricated," Mahoney responds.

"I think both should be re-interviewed," Corrigan suggests.

"Does that mean you think we should reopen the investigation?"

"Absolutely," Corrigan replies.

"My take as well," Mahoney says as he hands the file back to Corrigan. "Why make that a topic of discussion at our staff meeting this afternoon? Can't we just seek the approval of Commander Richards?"

"We can, but there are political ramifications. I don't want it to appear I have sour grapes over Donovan's acquittal and am seeking vengeance. I just find it odd that Nikki Palmer, who testified in Donovan's murder trial, was a key witness to Prescott's drowning."

WHEN CORRIGAN PROPOSES reopening the investigation of Prescott's suspect drowning, Richards is in attendance and gives his stamp of approval.

After the meeting, Richards pulls Corrigan aside and says, "After the acquittal in the first degree murder case, Cromwell met with the

Chief and complained about our shoddy investigation and the time and money wasted in pursuing a lost cause. My suggestion is that you schedule a meeting with Cromwell and get his take before embarking upon what very well could be another lost cause."

AT THE MEETING with Cromwell, Corrigan provides Cromwell with copies of the investigative reports. After Cromwell has reviewed and compared the reports, it is apparent they share the same skepticism concerning Cameron Donovan. Cromwell looks up and, raising his brows asks, "Are you considering both Palmer and Donovan suspects or is Palmer just a pawn in Donovan's hands like she was at Donovan's murder trial?"

"Hard to tell," Corrigan responds. "However, it is clear Donovan is the 'big fish,' and one we're really after. Palmer appears to be more of an unwitting participant. After all, she didn't appear to be involved in Donovan's plagiarism scheme and certainly didn't benefit from it."

"What I had suggested to the Chief was that, where the evidence is deficient, the grand jury is an effective vehicle in not only testing the waters but obtaining evidence that is otherwise unobtainable."

"A 'for instance?'"

"Granting Nikki Palmer immunity and having her testify before the grand jury. Otherwise, if she is a suspect she can invoke her Fifth Amendment rights and refuse to answer. If she refuses to answer, after she has been granted immunity, she can be held in contempt and fined or imprisoned."

"What if she lies before the grand jury?"

"Since she is placed under oath, lies regarding material matters are considered perjury and a felony under the laws of most states, including ours."

"What happens if Nikki sticks to her story and claims Prescott's drowning was accidental?"

"Well, we don't have a body to examine and prove otherwise and in the absence of something to the contrary, the grand jury won't have any basis to indict."

"And if she recants her story and incriminates both Donovan and herself, what then?"

"If that happens, you can file charges for any of Donovan's criminal acts, but not for Miss Palmer's. If the grant of immunity is structured right, she couldn't be prosecuted for anything connected with her testimony, including giving false information to police."

"What if she sticks to her story that the drowning was accidental or that Donovan acted in self-defense, can we still charge Donovan with giving false information to police?"

"Giving false information is a misdemeanor, and I'm not sure it would be worth all the effort and expense. What would be the benefit?"

"At least Donovan would end up with some conviction," Corrigan responds.

"Hardly seems worth the effort," Cromwell says. "If that is all you're after, then you're wasting my time."

"What's your advice?"

"Bring Miss Palmer in and re-interview her. If she sticks to her story and you don't think she's lying, then drop it. If you think she's lying and Prescott's death was due to some criminal agency, then call me and we'll grant her immunity and bring her before the grand jury."

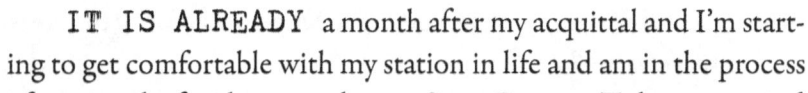

IT IS ALREADY a month after my acquittal and I'm starting to get comfortable with my station in life and am in the process of putting the finishing touches on *Sweet Revenge.* To keep my mind sharp and earn some extra money, I have been writing and selling articles and short stories to several small newspapers.

That having been said, I'm startled when I receive a call from Penwell.

"Detective Blake Corrigan of the Coral Cove Police Department came by my office and said because he thought I might still be representing you, he wanted my permission to interview you. Apparently, they have reopened the Prescott drowning investigation and have some follow-up question to ask."

"They just don't give up, do they?"

"Apparently not. Corrigan still has some kind of axe to grind with you."

"I assume they've also contacted Nikki."

"I didn't ask and they didn't say. However, it is only logical that they would do so."

"I'll be talking to her today and will ask."

"Before this all gets out of hand, I would suggest you plan a trip to Coral Cove and meet with me; the sooner the better."

"What's a good time for you?"

"Friday at 2:00 p.m."

"See you then."

I **NO MORE** than hang up with Penwell when I receive the distress call from Nikki.

"I thought everything was behind us," Nikki says.

"Apparently not," I reply. "You must have received the same call I did."

"I've not called him back but the message was to the effect that the Prescott drowning case has been reopened and Corrigan wants to re-interview me."

"Corrigan wants to re-interview me as well. I meet with Penwell on Friday and will have a better idea of what this is all about."

"What do you suppose?"

"Corrigan was not happy with the verdict and won't be happy until I'm behind bars. He'll do anything and everything to make my life miserable. It's me he is after, not you. He'll not leave any stone unturned until he has his way."

"What do you suggest I do?"

"Stall until after I meet with Penwell. Then we'll have a better idea."

———————

NOT WANTING NIKKI to fret or get thrown under the bus, I call Penwell and ask what advice he has for Nikki.

"Unfortunately, I cannot represent Nikki," Penwell says. "That would be a conflict of interest. However, I can give you the name of an attorney that you can pass on to her who would be in her price range and has the expertise to duel with the best. His name is Kent Moorhouse and his offices are just down the street from mine. If you would like, I can give him a call and an introduction."

"Would there be any problem if my family helped her with the fees?"

"None that I can see. In fact, it would be a noble gesture considering the circumstances and who the real target of Corrigan's wrath and investigation is."

———————

AS SOON AS I hang up with Penwell, I call Dad and advise him of the most recent development and the need to help Nikki with her separate attorney's fees.

"Before you leave for Coral Cove on Friday, come by my office. I presume the retainer fee will be $25,000 for each so I'll give you two checks," Dad says. "one for you and one for Nikki."

Living away from home since the acquittal has its benefits. When I want seclusion, I have it and when I want to interact with family, I'm always welcome. Surprisingly, I spend most of my time back home with my parents.

After I hang up with Dad, I immediately call Nikki.

"In light of the recent events, it's evident we both need legal representation. Since Penwell can't represent both of us, he's recommended Kent Moorhouse, an attorney located just down the street from his office."

"I know him! He goes to the same church I do," Nikki says. "Recently, he gave a seminar on wills and estates and I talked to him afterwards about doing my will. I like him."

"That's wonderful that you're acquainted with him. See if you can make an appointment with him sometime Friday afternoon."

"I have his card and I'll give him a call."

"I will be driving up to Coral Cove to meet with Penwell at 2:00. Afterwards, we could have lunch at the *Blue Dolphin* if you like."

"The *Blue Dolphin?* That brings back memories," Nikki says.

"Yes—pleasant ones, in fact." My heart skips a beat, maybe... I push those thoughts back for the present and rush on, "Oh, by the way, Dad will be picking up the attorney's fees for your representation..."

Nikki cuts me off, "He doesn't have to do that."

"He wants to," I reassure her. "Believe me, he can afford it. I will bring a check made payable to you and you can either deposit the check and write one to Moorhouse, or you can just endorse the check over to him."

A few minutes later Nikki calls back. "I made an appointment with Kent Moorhouse on Friday at 2:00. Apparently, Penwell had already alerted him that I would be calling."

"Awesome! I've never met him but Penwell gave him a glowing recommendation. I'll pick you up at 11:00 if that works."

WHEN I PICK Nikki up, she seems tense. "I'm a little nervous," Nikki says.

"Me too," I admit.

"Corrigan has something up his sleeve," Nikki says, "he's obviously trying to pit us against each other."

"Nikki, you have to recant your story and tell the truth. I'm prepared to do the same. Before, we worried our story would sound contrived and wanted to avoid telling how Prescott drugged us and tried to kill us."

"Yes, I remember. We even talked about his celebrity status and our nothing status, just a couple of college kids."

"Exactly. In retrospect, I think a blood test for the presence of drugs would have proven our story. Unfortunately, that's hindsight and now it doesn't matter. The simple truth is that, when I grabbed Prescott's gun hand after he pushed you over the railing, he lost his balance and we both tumbled into the ocean. Otherwise, we wouldn't be here to tell about it."

Nikki looks over at me with questioning eyes, "Are you sure that's what you want me to do?"

I reassure her, "Absolutely! The worst that can happen is that we will be cited for giving false information to the authorities—a minor infraction." Then, trying to maintain a positive attitude, I add, "Regardless what the consequences, we have to tell the truth. That's something I have learned the hard way."

"I know we're not responsible for Prescott's death," Nikki says.

"On the contrary, you tried to rescue him and made a valiant effort to do so even against all odds. Not only that, but you saved my life!"

"I'd do it again, a thousand times over," Nikki says and squeezes my arm.

"The truth will set us free," I say, knowing that our goals are the same and that justice is on our side.

We enjoy the lunch and feel relief and contentment in each other's company. On the business side, we both agree to tell our respective attorneys everything and follow their advice. We also agree not to say much over the phone or to anyone who may be a potential witness.

Later, when I pick Nikki up after meeting with our respective attorneys, we compare notes as I drive her home and when we part, both of us realize that our resolve will be severely tested, and pray that right will overcome might and justice will triumph in the end.

WHEN PENWELL MET with Corrigan at the CCPD, Penwell said he advised Corrigan that he still represents me. Penwell related that Corrigan bristled and asked, "Is your client afraid of the truth?" Penwell went on to say that he told Corrigan, "My client has nothing to hide and, on the contrary, wants to elaborate on his prior statement. Apparently, the investigation was pretty shoddy. It's my advice that before he talks to you, he has a chance to review his statement and have an understanding of what it is you're seeking and for what cause. Also, when the time comes, I will want to be present and record your questions and his responses."

"Fair enough," Corrigan apparently replied. He then exited the room and came back with a photocopy of Officer Cummings' report outlining my statement the night Prescott drowned. "As you can see, the statement was pretty general. There are some unanswered questions we have so that we can close the file on this one."

"Provide me with a list of your questions," Penwell said, "and I will see you get the answers."

"We'll still need to talk to Mr. Donovan," Corrigan said. "Nothing mysterious."

I'M SCHEDULED TO meet with Penwell the following Wednesday. I have lunch with Nikki beforehand and tell her about Penwell's meeting with Corrigan. She listens intently, then placing her crossed arms on the table, she tells me about her attorney's meeting with Corrigan.

"When Kent said he had advised against me making another statement, Corrigan threatened to have a grand jury subpoena issued requiring me to appear and testify. Kent said, being my attorney, he would demand to be present and would instruct me to invoke my Fifth Amendment rights against self-incrimination."

I reach across the table and squeeze Nikki's arm, "If I were issued a subpoena, I would invoke the same rights."

"Anyway," Nikki says and smiles at me before continuing, "Corrigan's tone softened somewhat and he said I was not a target. When asked who the target was, Corrigan stated it was you. He offered immunity in exchange for my testimony assuming, of course, that I would recant my prior statement and incriminate you." Nikki frowns, then continues, "Corrigan intimated that you had something to do with Prescott's death."

Stunned, I respond, "Prescott drowned, plain and simple."

"You and I know that. What Corrigan doesn't know is that you acted in self-defense and in my defense. By the way, you are always giving me credit for saving your life. Actually, if it hadn't been for you trying to disarm Prescott, neither of us would be here today."

I nod, still numbed by this new turn of events. I say, "Penwell surmises Corrigan thinks I did Prescott in to claim authorship of *Beguiled.* You and I both know that was not the case. It was only after Prescott's death that the thought even crossed my mind. Plagiarism is bad enough but to kill someone to become famous is not and never will be in my DNA."

"If I do testify, Cam," Nikki's voice now sounds more authoritative, "that's exactly what I will tell the grand jury—not because I care for you, but because it is the truth."

AFTER NIKKI TESTIFIED before the grand jury, Corrigan became even more desperate. He had me tailed and I suspect he had my phone tapped. He interviewed my friends and even threatened to call my parents in to testify before the grand jury. If Cromwell hadn't resisted, I'm sure that would have happened.

In private, Penwell met with Cromwell and told him that enough was enough and that I was being harassed by Corrigan. Penwell and Cromwell entered into a pact that, unbeknownst to the world, if I took and passed a polygraph administered by the Florida Bureau of Investigation, he would insure that the harassment ended. Cromwell said he and the Chief were close friends, and, in fact, distant relatives, and that, if Corrigan persisted, he would be fired.

WHEN THE POLYGRAPH results were released and I was told by Penwell that I had passed, I called Nikki and my parents, in that order, to announce the good news. When the grand jury returned a 'no true-bill,' meaning no indictment had been issued, both Cromwell and the CCPD closed their files. When I learned that Corrigan was no longer a member of the CCPD, I guessed he was given the option of retiring or being fired.

EPILOGUE

Almost three years have passed and I'm back to where it all began; sitting on the redwood deck of my parents' home. As I reflect, I find myself preoccupied by my blunder in plagiarizing Prescott's novel, a deception that still plagues me today. If only I could turn back the clock and right the wrongs that affected those I love the most. Perhaps it is not too late. What's that old saying, "Today is the first day of the rest of my life."

Dad and I are going to take *Pizzazz* out for a spin this morning. I look up as he approaches. Dad would like to dive but his doctor, over Dad's protests, *strongly* advises him against it. He has recovered from his heart attack and is now in what he likes to call, 'better shape than ever.'

"Ready, Son?" Dad asks, as he carefully scans the sea and the sky. "Looks like a good day for a little jaunt out on the briny. I've missed our time together, so let's get movin', we're burnin' daylight."

"I'm on it," I reply, and we descend the steps and stroll toward the jetty where *Pizzazz* is moored.

Once we're aboard the craft, I take the copilot seat next to Dad and we head for open waters. The fresh air and occasional spray of salt water refresh me.

Dad looks over at me, "Why don't you drive for a while," he says and we switch places. When we do, I notice that he appears to be melancholy as he continues, "Cam, if anything good can come from having a heart attack, it's that I've learned to slow down and enjoy the ride." Then looking up at the swarm of squawking gulls descending upon us, he quips, "Hell, I've even learned to tolerate those damn buzzards."

I smile and nod. I fear if I try to talk the tears that brim my eyes will reveal how fragile I am and I don't want to upset Dad. I'm once again steeped in the guilt of having put my parents through the rigors of a murder trial. However, I am, and always will be, grateful that they *are* my parents.

Mom and Dad were present in the courtroom every day of my trial and beside me all the way. Just their presence gave me the courage I desperately needed to survive. Their eyes conveyed their love and understanding and buoyed me up when I felt myself going under. Being falsely charged with the murder of Lisette Kingston, and suspected involvement in Prescott's drowning, not to mention the added shame of having committed plagiarism, was almost more than I could bear. I try hard to put it all behind me.

ALTHOUGH AT TRIAL I was exonerated of the murder charge, I still faced the civil and possibly the criminal consequences regarding plagiarism. Penwell and I met with Hannah, Prescott's sister and sole heir, before she returned to Sydney. She indicated she would not pursue the plagiarism charge or sue for copyright infringement if we assigned the copyright of *Jeopardy* to her and disgorged the profits I had obtained from the publisher. She also wanted written assurance I would denounce my claim as being the author of either *Jeopardy* or *Beguiled* and would lay no claims thereto in the future. This we wholeheartedly agreed to do.

Penwell immediately contacted the publisher, Keeley House, and set the wheels in motion to effectuate the assignment of any and all of my rights in *Jeopardy* and to rename the novel *Beguiled,* including changing the name of the author and the names of the characters. For all intents and purposes, *Jeopardy* ceased to be.

AFTER ALL THAT'S happened, and to quote Dad's logic, "if anything good can come from this," it's that Nikki forgave me and we're back together. In fact, Nikki asked Mom to plan our wedding. I remember Nikki saying, "...if I leave it up to my Dad, we'd probably have a Scottish bash at Calhoun's, all of us decked out in kilts, dancing to a bagpipe and getting tipsy on grog..."

I watched Mom light up like a Christmas tree when Nikki asked her to plan the wedding. Not having a daughter of her own, Mom embraced the opportunity with gusto and has put her whole heart into the project. Although the "main event" is over two months away, almost every room in our house is cluttered with wedding paraphernalia and...we have many rooms. Mom's days are filled with ensuring every detail is addressed. It is agreed that Nikki and I will be married at St. Joseph's Cathedral in Key West and the reception held at *The Key Astoria.* The guest list looks like a small country's phonebook. Judging from the amount of RSVPs that keep pouring in, most everyone is planning to attend.

OH, BY THE way, did I mention that after I was exonerated at trial, Charlotte Hudson from Keeley House contacted me. The publisher had been sitting on *Sweet Revenge* pending the outcome of my trial, a trial that received nationwide coverage similar to that of O.J. Simpson's. When all of the facts of my case were exposed and it became public knowledge that I had written a novel unraveling the whole sordid mess, Keeley House rushed to publish *Sweet Revenge*. Apparently, the plagiarism was forgiven if not forgotten when my trial received nationwide attention tantamount to millions of dollars' worth of free advertising. The royalty advance accompanying the contract from Keeley House for rights to publish *Sweet Revenge* was a check for $100,000. "...and that's just for starters..." Charlotte said the day she called.

I keep quoting Dad's logic, probably because I've learned he's a wise man. "If anything good has come from it, it's having *Sweet Revenge* on the New York Times Bestseller list for six weeks and counting." *Sweet Revenge* instantly shot to the top of the charts the week it was released and it doesn't show signs of slowing down anytime soon. The monthly $10,000 royalty checks keep rolling in and I'm back on top of the world. My parents refuse to let me repay the lawyers' fees they anted up for me. *Some day, some way.*

EACH NIGHT BEFORE I drift off, I pray for forgiveness and say a prayer of thanks for all the blessings I've received. During the time I was experiencing the molding process, I wasn't sure there was a God. However, having witnessed the miracles He's worked in my life, I now have no doubt whatsoever that He is real. The God I've come to know is loving, generous, merciful, and most of all, forgiving. We are even instructed by the Master of the Universe to "... forgive those who trespass against us..." I shudder when I think of how differently things could have turned out. I realize that I'm still a work in progress because, try as I may to emulate His commands, the forgiving part has been a challenge—especially when it comes to forgiving myself.

MANEUVERING *PIZZAZZ* THROUGH familiar channels, I look out across the Atlantic as we speed along on the ocean's calm surface. When I glance over at Dad, I notice him readjusting his *Marlin's* baseball cap, and pushing it back on his head. That gesture alerts me that something serious is coming so I brace myself.

Dad finally says, "You're unusually quiet, Cam. I've known you all your life and I recognize the sign that something's troubling you. Care to share?"

I shake my head. I don't want Dad to know that I'm thinking about Prescott. Prescott's body was never recovered, and as I scan the ocean knowing his remains are out there somewhere, I can't help but feel his spirit. I also remember something Prescott said the day we met: "Be careful what you write. An author may die, but his words will endure forever." I also remember him saying, "Your words are your legacy and based on what you write, you will be judged."

ABOUT the AUTHORS

Judith Blevins' whole professional life has been centered in and around the courts and the criminal justice system. Her experience in having been a court clerk and having served under five consecutive district attorneys in Grand Junction, Colorado, has provided the fodder for her novels. She has had a daily dose of mystery, intrigue and courtroom drama over the years and her novels share all with her readers.

Carroll Multz, a trial lawyer for over forty years, a former two-term district attorney, assistant attorney general, and judge, has been involved in cases ranging from municipal courts to and including the United States Supreme Court. His high profile cases have been reported in the *New York Times*, *Redbook Magazine* and various police magazines. He was one of the attorneys in the Columbine Copycat Case that occurred in Fort Collins, Colorado, in 2001 that was featured by Barbara Walters on ABC's *20/20*. Now retired, he is an Adjunct Professor at Colorado Mesa University in Grand Junction, Colorado, teaching law-related courses at both the graduate and undergraduate levels.

www.ingramcontent.com/pod-product-compliance
Lightning Source LLC
Chambersburg PA
CBHW030341180626
46812CB00007B/2716